D1255273

Murder Confounded

By the same author:

AN EVIL HOUR
THE STALKING HORSE
MURDER MOVIE

Lloyd and Hill Mysteries

A PERFECT MATCH
THE MURDERS OF MRS AUSTIN & MRS BEALE
THE OTHER WOMAN

RODERIC JEFFRIES

Murder Confounded

St. Martin's Press
New York

Library of Congress Cataloging-in-Publication Data

Jeffries, Roderic.
Murder confounded / Roderic Jeffries.
p.   cm.
ISBN 0-312-09877-4 (hardcover)
1. Alvarez, Enrique (Fictitious character)—Fiction.   2. Police-
-Spain—Majorca—Fiction.   3. Majorca (Spain)—Fiction.   I. Title.
PR6060.E43M78   1993
823'.914—dc20   93-8978   CIP

First published in Great Britain by HarperCollins*Publishers*

First U.S. Edition: September 1993

10 9 8 7 6 5 4 3 2 1

CHAPTER 1

It had been said that were Brand to arrive at the Pearly Gates to find them wide open and a welcome banner strung above, he would still wait for a formal invitation, engraved, not printed, before entering. He asked, in his surprisingly deep voice since he was a small man: 'Is everything in order?' He had an egg-shaped head, made eggier by growing baldness.

'Couldn't be anything else with you in charge, Mr Brand.'

He smiled briefly to conceal his distaste for such unctuousness, for he tried to treat every student who passed through Hawdon Hall Rehabilitation Centre with the same courteousness. Hickey, a con man, had for some years specialized in defrauding newly bereaved widows; when at last the police had gathered enough evidence to charge him, he had offered to provide incriminating evidence on fellow criminals provided he was sent to Hawdon Hall rather than prison; since the information would, among other things, enable the police to arrest the members of a gang which had carried out several brutal armed robberies, authority had very reluctantly agreed. Brand wasn't certain whether he despised Hickey more for his mean thefts or his ready betrayals, but no one would have guessed from his manner the contempt he felt for the other. 'I've asked you here to stress two things as well as to say goodbye. You must realize that you will not find life easy. Yet when you're driven through the gates this morning, you can no longer call on us for help; from that moment, every connection between you and this Centre will be severed.'

'I do understand that.'

'Experience suggests that loneliness will be your greatest enemy because it can distort your judgement. Loneliness may suggest that provided you take care, it will be safe to make brief contact with your past. You have to remember that no such contact can ever be safe.'

Hickey spoke with great earnestness. 'I'm going to keep as far away from my past, Mr Brand, as it's possible to get.' He coughed, spoke haltingly. 'I don't quite know how to put this, but I feel that from now on I have to lead a life which proves all the trouble you and the staff have gone to has been worthwhile.'

'Good,' said Brand. He thought that his and his staff's efforts were much more likely to be proved a total waste of time. 'Then all that is left for me to do is to wish you a good life.' He stood, came round the desk, and shook hands.

After Hickey had left, Brand picked up the folder from his desk and crossed to the door behind his chair. Beyond was a walk-in strong-room, the massive door of which was secured by two digital combination locks. Rules said that the combinations must be changed once a month. He changed them at nine o'clock on the first of each month, even when the first fell on a Sunday. He punched out the numbers, pulled open the door, stepped inside. On the shelves were stored the confidential files of all students, past and present. It was a source of satisfaction to him that from the day he had been appointed chief executive, only the person concerned and he could possibly know what was in each file.

He put Hickey's file on one of the bottom shelves, picked up Gore's from the top left-hand one. He left the strong-room and shut the door, scrambled the combinations. Since he would be returning to the strong-room within the hour, the only access to it was through his office, and as he would not be leaving that, this would have seemed to be an unnecessary precaution to most. But the rules called for the strong-room to be secured when not actually in use.

He returned to his seat behind the desk, stared at the file. Franklin Gore. Try as he had, he'd been unable to develop any sense of rapport with the other and that disturbed him because Gore was a brave and honest man who had served in the police. Unfortunately, their first meeting had set a pattern he'd been unable to change. He always went to the station to meet the incoming student and drove him back to the Centre and none of the other staff was allowed to have the slightest contact with that student until given his new name; then, only he could connect past and present. At the station, Gore—who'd clearly been drinking heavily—had been off-hand; on the ten-minute drive, sullenly silent; in the office, offensive.

'The first thing we have to do,' Brand had said after they'd arrived, 'is decide on your new name.' Then, in order to introduce a note of informality, he'd made the usual joke. 'I claim I've assisted in more christenings than any parson.'

'Then I hope you don't favour total immersion.'

He'd managed a smile. 'Obviously, the name you choose must have no direct or indirect connection with your past one.'

'I don't give a damn what I'm called.'

'Then how about Franklin Gore?'

It was hours later that, with a sense of guilt, he'd remembered Franklin Gore had been the obnoxious class bully at school . . .

There was a knock on the door and Sarah entered, bringing morning coffee. 'I've not put any biscuits on the tray because you said yesterday that you've given up eating 'em.'

'Not by choice, but because of avoirdupois. Or, as I suppose I should say in an era of Europeanism, metricdupois.' It was obvious she had not understood his little word play.

'Sarah, I'm afraid there were two spelling errors in that last letter you typed.'

'Oh dear!' She was fresh-faced, a little overweight, and carefree.

'Try and remember, it's I before E, except after C.'

'We never did much spelling at school.'

'So I've gathered. I suggest you make a closer friend of your dictionary.'

'I'll do just that,' she said, before she left.

He knew that the dictionary and she would remain near total strangers. The modern generation didn't seem to worry about things which had once been important. He added one spoonful of sugar to the coffee and a little milk, lit a cigarette. Even though he only smoked four a day, his wife continually tried to persuade him to give up this vice. More than once, he'd reminded her of Jean-Pierre Courien's words: 'A man without a vice is like bouillabaisse without racasse.'

He finished the coffee, stubbed out the cigarette, opened the file and skimmed through the papers inside to refresh his memory. Then he checked the time, phoned Sarah to ask if Gore were waiting, asked her to show him in.

Gore said, ''Morning,' as if even that much of a civility was an effort.

'Please sit down . . . I've asked you in not only to say goodbye and good luck, but also to stress one or two important facts. Things are not going to be easy for you after you leave here. Loneliness represents a danger . . .'

'The onion man's been over all that.'

'The onion man?'

'Blackeley. Forever repeating himself.'

Not inappropriate, Brand thought; he must remember to tell his wife. 'I do think you need to take things a little more seriously than you would appear to do. Severe emotional isolation can be a traumatic experience . . .'

'I very much doubt I'll be any more emotionally isolated than when I was working undercover.'

'Perhaps not, but I would suggest that there will be a significant difference. Then, you could look forward to an end to your isolation, now there can be no guarantee. You must face the fact that loneliness—nostalgic loneliness—can strike long after you believe this to be impossible and imbue you with a desperate urge to make contact with some part of the past. Accepting the possibility will make you more able to overcome it.'

'It's accepted,' said Gore, with offhand indifference.

Advice is seldom welcome; and those who want it the most always like it the least. 'Very well. Now, there's the problem of money.'

'Provided I receive it, there's no problem.'

'It has been paid into an account at the Banco de Castilla in Andorra la Vella. I gather the bank is no stranger to the more unorthodox financial transactions and has therefore evolved a formula to make certain no one but you can activate the account even though you have had no previous contact with them. The procedure is . . .' He opened the folder, found the paper he wanted, read. 'In a moment, over the phone, you and a member of the bank decide on a reference. I provide you with an introductory letter in which is left a blank and in this you enter the agreed reference. When you present yourself at the bank, with your passport of course, you hand in this letter and it will open the account to you. I will telephone the bank now. After I've left the room, you will speak to their representative and decide on the reference you wish to use.'

'Why bother to leave?'

'I prefer not to be privy to such details.' Brand lifted the receiver of the outside phone, dialled International, then the bank's number. The call was answered initially by a man who spoke Catalan, but who switched to reasonable English. He asked Brand to wait.

'Hullo, Mr Brand. Pablo Pons speaking.'

Brand returned the greeting, then identified the account number.

'The money's on deposit at the best rate obtainable for non-term.'

'I'm going to ask Mr Franklin Gore to speak to you to decide on the requisite reference which will be included in our G4 introductory letter. Would you hold on, please?' He put the receiver down, nodded at Gore, left.

In the next room, he said to Sarah: 'Would you prepare a G4, please?'

'Yes, Mr Brand.' She opened one of the drawers of the desk, brought out a printed master form, laid that by the side of the typewriter into which she wound two sheets of paper with a carbon, began to type. She stopped, looked up. 'I'm afraid I've forgotten. Was it I before E or E before I?'

'I before E. E rhymes with C.'

'That's smart!'

It would have to be very smart to improve her spelling.

Gore came through from the inner office. 'Everything's fixed, so all I have to do for a good time is knock twice and ask for Dolly.'

Sarah giggled. Brand, who believed that a gentleman did not make a smutty innuendo in front of a lady, said: 'Are you packed?'

'Down to the last odd sock.'

'Then as soon as Miss Bingham has finished typing the letter, she can give it to you and you can fill in the blank. Then she'll ask someone to drive you to the station.' He held out his hand. 'I'll say goodbye now as I have a busy morning left. Good luck.' He was not surprised when Gore shook hands with unnecessary force. But he had a strong grip and gave as good as he received. It was the first time he'd seen the slightest sign of respect on the other's face.

CHAPTER 2

The expatriate community were agreed on only two facts —the Mallorquin way of doing anything was bound to be cock-eyed and Sir Donald Macadie was of the old school.

Six feet one tall, back ramrod straight, hair still thick, he had dark brown eyes that could twinkle or regard with frosty disapproval any word or action that offended his standards, an eagle's beak for a nose, and a mouth that could laugh with such freedom that it made others laugh even when they didn't really know why.

There were, of course, some who did not perceive 'of the old school' to be a compliment. For them, his easy manner was condescension and his often expressed wish for the estate to reach its thousandth anniversary as the height of snobbish stupidity. And to such people, his marriage to a woman half his age funded endless jibes about wasted assets.

The family seat was in Shropshire and if an heir lived until 2068, part of the land would have been in the family's possession for a thousand years. He loved the English countryside above everything else in the world and had he not suffered with increasing severity from asthma would never have moved abroad, even if to do so would ease the tax burden. But after Honor had died, he'd met Vivien . . .

Honor. County, and possessed of as strong a love of country and tradition as he. Socially, she had been an ideal wife. She'd known whom to sit on the right-hand side of her husband and herself when they were entertaining at dinner a high court judge and his wife, a life peer and his wife, a bishop and his wife, and a financier and the third bimbo of the year. She could manage staff, even though her manner was sometimes tinged with the touch of autocracy so often found in people who had always known wealth. She could size up a hunter's potential with a look. Sadly, however, physically she had been far from an ideal wife (a fact he'd tried, and failed, to hide from himself during her lifetime), but she had submitted, no doubt consoling herself with thoughts on duty, the Empire, and the sad lack of parthenogenesis among mammals. Then she'd suffered a prolapsed womb, had had to have a hysterectomy which had left her an invalid for months, and this had decided her that after all she'd endured (the indignities she'd had to suffer before she'd called a halt to the infertility tests) no one could reasonably expect her to continue to submit to primal practices.

One morning she'd been thrown from her horse when it put a leg in a rabbit hole. Scorning any headgear other than the traditional velvet hat, the crown of her head had been crushed and she'd died that night. The shock of her death had caused him such severe bouts of asthma that twice he'd had to be rushed into hospital, on each occasion spending hours in an oxygen tent. It was after he'd recovered from the second attack that his specialist had advised him to give up the struggle to live in a climate designed to cause and exacerbate respiratory diseases and to find somewhere where the sun shone, there was little grass or other wind-borne pollen, and air pollution was negligible. He had not taken the advice. Deeply depressed by the loss of his wife and the lack of an heir, his attitude had been, why bother?

Too intelligent and too active to lead a meaningless life for long, some eighteen months after Honor's death he'd decided to carry out a project that had rested in the back of his mind for years—to write a history of the family from the date of the first grant of land. (The role a historian should play had caused him some concern. Was he in honour bound to report all he knew? Or could

he legitimately suppress a fact if this had absolutely no
bearing on events which proceeded from it? The fact that
Oswald Macadie had paid James I four hundred and
twenty guineas for his baronetcy in 1622 had not altered
by one jot the course of the family's history; but did it
perhaps appear to tarnish the honour?) His work in long-
hand had run to hundreds of pages, so he'd spoken to his
land agent to ask if the other could suggest someone who
would be glad of part-time typing.

Vivien. Attractive, smart, hard-working; always cheerful
despite the fact that her husband had died the previous
year, leaving almost as many debts as happy memories. A
woman of contradictions. Quiet, modest, and retiring; jok-
ing, teasing, and with eyes that could suggest wanton pleasures. For several days her midnight-black hair would be
fashioned with stern simplicity, then it would tumble about
her oval face with sophisticated abandon. Normally she
used little make-up and wore decorous clothes; occasionally, she liberally applied eye shadow, powder, lipstick,
swapped My Sin for her usual eau-de-Cologne, and wore
clothes which revealed much while still concealing all.

By chapter four, he was regretting the difference in their
ages; by chapter nine, he was doubting that this mattered
as much as was often said; by chapter eleven . . .

He had stumbled when near her desk and in recovering
his balance had inadvertently brushed her right breast with
his hand. He'd immediately apologized. 'Who's fussed?'
she'd asked. A kind way of easing his embarrassment at the
thought she might have misunderstood; or a way of saying,
what makes you think I want an apology?

She'd had to ask him to decipher a paragraph in the
twelfth chapter, written in an even more spidery hand than
usual. In 1624, Sir Oswald Macadie had been shown his
first born. 'By God's favour, he's a strapping Macadie!'

'Sir,' the midwife had said nervously, 'she's a girl.' 'The poxy devil it is? Send it back, for I've no use of it.'

'Hardly a thoughtful husband!' Vivien had commented.

Macadie, standing by the side of the desk, had said pedantically: 'Don't judge too harshly. He'd become very wealthy and reached a high position in society. The doctors had told him that after contracting measles at the age of thirty he'd be sterile and so when his wife became pregnant, he regarded that as a miracle. When the child turned out to be a daughter, the wonder turned into something rather less.'

'But of course!'

They'd laughed.

'He wasn't to know,' continued Macadie, 'that three sons would follow in the next five years.'

'It's funny, isn't it, how often life has a joker up its sleeve?'

'You've suffered several?'

'Who hasn't?'

He'd invited her to dinner that night. She'd insisted on returning home to change, despite his assurance that that was totally unnecessary, and when the Filipino butler had shown her into the Trafalgar Room, he'd been irresistibly reminded (to both his annoyance and his amusement) of the description of Sir Horace Macadie's Irish mistress. 'A very lusty female, wearing modesty with difficulty and causing every man to wonder if her secret delights were as perseveringly cultivated as her obvious ones.'

The dinner had been a great success.

He had asked her to marry him but, since he was a man who observed a strict code, not before he had carefully explained that because Honor had failed to conceive, both she and he had begun tests for infertility and he had discovered that he was infertile. Therefore, Vivien could never bear his child. She had shown a keen grasp of essentials and had spent far more time commiserating with him over the impossibility of his having an heir than in her delight at accepting his offer.

It was after their marriage that she said he really should accept the medical advice he'd been given and move abroad.

'No.'

'For your own sake, my darling, you've got to try to find better health than you suffer in this country.'

'I've been as fit as a fiddle since I met you.'

'Do you call yesterday afternoon, being fit?'

'That . . . that attack was caused by something unusual.'

'I couldn't bear to lose the wonderful happiness I've found just because you wouldn't listen to the doctors.' She knew that he was prepared to suffer for his love of Stowton Place, but not to make her suffer for her love of him.

The decision to move abroad having been taken, their destination had to be decided. He'd tapped his fingers on the arm of the chair, as he often did when uncertain. 'Where shall we go?'

'I've always dreamt of living on an island in the Mediterranean.'

'There are any number of Greek islands which are said to be very attractive, but I believe there are problems with owning property in that country despite the Common Market. Then there's Sardinia and that development— wasn't it started by the Aga Khan?—which is said to be very pleasant.'

'Isn't that where an Englishman's daughter some years ago was kidnapped and held to ransom?'

'Now you mention it, I believe it was. Presumably, to finance a local group whose aim was Sardinia for the sardines.'

'Really, Donald, that's not even up to fourth-form humour! . . . I don't know that I'd feel easy living somewhere where that sort of thing had happened.'

'I suppose if one's to be realistic, it can happen anywhere.'

'But having done so once, surely it's more likely to do so again?'

'Lightning never strikes twice.'

'According to the *Guinness Book of Records*, there's an American who's been struck seven times.'

'To be struck once may be regarded as a misfortune; to be struck seven times looks like carelessness.'

'Stop being difficult. Why don't we go to Majorca?'

'Good God!'

'I'm not suggesting Sodom.'

'Being old-fashioned, I wouldn't know about that. But if the press is anything to go by, Majorca is about to sink under the weight of concrete and lager louts.'

'Have you ever been there?'

'No.'

'Then reserve your scorn for when you have.' She stood, crossed to his chair and fondled his cheek. 'I went there on my first honeymoon.'

'Rose-coloured spectacles.'

'Shut up! Parts of it are Grottsville. Other parts are so beautiful they grab you inside. What we have to do is find somewhere in the most beautiful part.'

'You don't think it might be more fun to look around? We could rent a place on a Greek island . . .'

'We have to be realistic as well as romantic. We probably could find an island outside the mainstream of tourism, but by definition that would mean it would be lacking facilities. God forbid you have another very severe asthma attack, but if you do, we must be close to first-class medical help.

It could take hours and hours to rush you to a decent hospital from an out-of-the-way place.'

'I suppose that is a point.'

'And another thing, we must be where it'll be simple to return here whenever you want to renew yourself.'

'Want to do what?'

'Don't you find in the estate the kind of reason for living that other people find in religion?'

'You amaze me.'

'May I never stop doing so.'

They rented a large villa and began their search for a home. They saw houses of great luxury, houses directly on the sea, houses with extensive views, but although he was forced to admit that his previous, all-embracing scorn for the island was totally unjustified, and despite her later, keen enthusiasm for several of them, he decided that this had to be one occasion when he did not accede to her wishes. They would explore somewhere else, somewhere where he could enjoy the feeling of space and freedom from neighbours who, however pleasant, gave the impression that they favoured plastic gnomes . . .

An employee of one of the estate agents arrived unheralded and announced in aggravated English that he was going to show them a unique property which had just come on the market.

'I'm sorry,' Macadie said, 'but we're not looking at anywhere else because we've decided not to settle on the island.'

'This castle, señor, is sufficient for a king.'

'I'm afraid I'm only a baronet.'

'Is impossible to talk about. Must see. You not see, you kill yourself.'

'I'm prepared to take that risk.'

Macadie had not realized that Mallorquin agents

charged so much commission that if there was even the slightest chance of a sale, the only way of getting rid of one was forcibly to eject him.

Son Termol. Reached by a six-kilometre dirt track that wound its way round one mountain and up two sides of another. Three houses, which stood on a flat crest. Views to the west, of the Sierra de Cala Roig; to the north, of the sea; to the east, of the spiny promontory of Parelona and of Llueso Bay; to the south, beyond the crests of lesser heights, the plain of Mestara.

Macadie, the wind fiddling with his hair, savoured the scene.

'Why are there three houses?' Vivien asked.

The agent smirked. 'Is built by Austrian count who likes very much the ladies. They not wish all to live together.'

Macadie said: 'Clearly, a man who held variety to be the spice of vice . . . How much land is there?'

'Two hundred and fifty hectares, señor.'

'Roughly where do the boundaries run?'

'Is all the land you look, right to sky.'

'I shouldn't have thought it could stretch quite that far,' he said, amused by the exaggeration.

'Wouldn't it be an idea to look at the inside of the houses?' suggested Vivien, in a tone of voice which made it clear she had not missed the exterior flaking plaster, broken shutters, missing panes of glass, and cracked tiles.

They went into the right-hand house. It looked as if vagrants had broken into it and lived there for a few months. 'My God, what an appalling mess!' she said.

'Perhaps some pesetas to reform,' admitted the agent. 'But no problem.'

When God had been wondering whether to create woman, a Mallorquin had advised, No problem.

*

Back in their rented house, Vivien had said: 'Are you serious? It would be like living in the bush.'

'I timed the drive back and it was only twenty-five minutes to the village. If you think about it, it takes twenty minutes to get from Stowton Place to Little Sowerbury . . . Have you ever before seen such a setting?'

'Who wants three houses?'

'One for us, one for the servants, and one for guests. Think of how much more agreeable it is to have guests if you can shut them out of your lives for so many hours each day.'

'If that's the way you think, why ask them in the first place?'

'In my experience, most guests ask themselves.'

'What's it going to cost to renovate the three houses?'

'I don't think we need worry too much about that side of things. Still, if you're so dead set against buying the property, we'll forget it.'

'I'm not dead set, darling, just trying to decide if it's a very sensible idea. We really would be on our own. It's hardly the kind of home where the neighbours drop in for coffee and a chat.'

'You make it sound even more attractive.'

'And you're being even more difficult! You know very well you're no misanthropist.'

'All right. I humbly confess. I've fallen in love with the place and so am even trying to capitalize on its drawbacks. To tell the truth, I fancy revelling on my own private Olympus.'

She could usually judge what course was likely to be the most beneficial in the long run. She stepped forward until she could rest her cheek against his. 'Then to hell with all the problems. We'll live on Olympus. But, darling Zeus, no swanning off after Leda.'

*

The builders promised faithfully that the work would be completed by September since it was the custom to tell a foreigner whatever it was that the foreigner most wanted to hear. They finally finished it the following March.

From the outside, the three rock-built houses had looked dour; now, with carefully planned extensions altering and smoothing their silhouettes, they had become merely solid. Inside, thanks to Vivien's natural flair for form and colour, they were warm and welcoming. Earth by the truckload had been brought up to form a garden; mature olive and palm trees were transplanted, flowerbeds designed, and a lawn of gamma grass set around the clover-leaf swimming-pool. It was enough to make the gods on Olympus jealous.

CHAPTER 3

Outside the kitchen of the hundred-and-fifty-year-old farm-house was an overhead vine which provided both shade and grapes. Verd and Alvarez sat at the rough wooden table set under this.

'They're stealing my tomatoes,' said Verd for the third time, a single tooth in front giving his words the hint of a whistle. 'It's them Frenchies down the road what's rented Gaspar's house.'

'Have you seen 'em at it?' Alvarez drank. The homemade wine held the taste of hot, dry earth and carried memories of his youth.

Verd did not answer the question. 'D'you know what they're paying? A hundred thousand!'

'Rents can be high in the summer.'

'But a hundred thousand!' Some said Verd was simple and that was why he was unable to understand the world had changed. The truth was, he was so scared of change that he had mentally to remain in the past if he were to survive the present. So he still believed a hundred pesetas to be a considerable sum of money. 'If they're so rich, why are they stealing my tomatoes?'

The obvious answer was that when tomatoes grew in such abundance within picking distance of the road, the French tourists had viewed them as they would had they been blackberries growing wild. They were not to know that fifty years before, when hunger had stalked the land, even blackberries growing wild had belonged to someone. Alvarez finished the wine.

Verd picked up the bottle and refilled both glasses.

They watched Verd's wife approach them between two

rows of sweet peppers. Her blunt face was lined and tanned by countless hours in the fields; her dress was patched and patched again; her shoes were on the point of disintegrating. As she passed to go into the house, she nodded at Alvarez, but did not speak.

Alvarez repeated the question. 'Have you seen the French picking your tomatoes?'

'No.'

'Then how can you be certain it's them?'

'They're the only foreigners living around here.'

Years ago, a man could leave his house unlocked in the morning and return in the evening to find nothing missing; now, it would be ransacked. For Verd, it was logical to blame the foreigners for this and every other disturbing change. 'I'll have a word with them,' Alvarez promised.

Verd's wife came out of the house and again passed in silence.

'I guess I'd better start moving.' Alvarez drained his glass.

'The bottle ain't empty.'

Life was about priorities.

As Alvarez walked into the house there was the nose-tingling smell of cooking and he hurried through to the kitchen. Dolores, sweating profusely, stood by the cooker, stirring the contents of a cazuela.

'Fabada?' he asked expectantly. 'With those special chorizos you found in the new supermarket which are nearly as good as the ones your cousins make?'

She stopped stirring, used an oven cloth to set a lid on the cazuela and lift it into the oven, then turned. 'You arrive home and immediately demand to know what there is to eat! Naturally you do not first ask how am I, or say how much it distresses you to see me slaving in a kitchen which has become a furnace.'

'Both Jaime and I have suggested that when it's this hot, you should give us cold meals . . .'

Hands on hips, handsome head held high, lustrous dark brown eyes sharp, she said: 'You imagine I would allow you to shame me by telling the village I do not cook for you?'

'But if you won't . . .' He stopped. She was a woman of emotions, not logic. Better to try to lessen her sense of resentment. 'Whatever you're cooking, it smells absolutely delicious.'

'Naturally.' She removed her hands from her hips. 'This is a small kitchen even when I'm permitted to have it to myself.'

He returned to the dining-room, which was also the family sitting-room, crossed to the ornately carved sideboard, opened the right-hand door and brought out a bottle of brandy and a tumbler. Then he heard the swish of the bead curtain across the front door and reached down for a second tumbler.

Jaime entered. 'Fill it up to the brim—my throat's drier than the Sahara. And don't go easy on the ice.'

'I haven't got that yet.'

Jaime went through to the kitchen. It was unfortunate that his first words were to ask his wife what was for lunch. As Alvarez listened to Dolores, he wondered why Spain was called a patriarchal society?

Jaime returned, without any ice. 'Why the hell didn't you warn me that she's in one of her moods?' he demanded in a low voice.

'I thought I'd managed to calm her down.'

'You'd have done better keeping your mouth shut, wouldn't you?'

Juan and Isabel arrived in a rush. Juan sniffed the air, then shouted through the kitchen doorway. 'What's for lunch?'

The two men waited expectantly.

'One of your favourites; fabada.'

'Great! I'm starving!'

'It's almost ready, so go and wash your hands. And if your father and uncle can leave the bottle alone long enough, ask them to lay the table.'

Alvarez looked at Jaime, then refilled their glasses.

The phone rang in the middle of the meal. Dolores, her manner less abrasive than it had been, looked across at Alvarez. 'At this sort of time, it has to be for you.'

His plate was piled high with a second helping of the delicious stew of beans, pork, chorizo, pepper, and garlic; he helped himself to a large spoonful before he went through to the front room.

Superior Chief Salas's secretary, who always sounded as if she had a mouthful of plums, said: 'You are to go to the Clinica Barón and speak to Dr Molina to discuss the nature of the injuries Señor Gore has suffered.'

'Does the señor come from Llueso?'

'He lives in Altobarí.'

'But that's the other end of the island. Surely this isn't a matter for me, but for whoever's inspector there . . .'

'Señor Gore does not speak Spanish and Inspector Fiol does not speak English. The superior chief says you are to make contact immediately.' She cut the connection, not bothering—any more than Salas would have done—to say goodbye.

He replaced the receiver. Immediately was an ambiguous word. To a Madrileño it meant one thing, because he was forever in a rush. To a Mallorquin, it meant something different since he had the sense to remember that the more one hurried, the easier it was to stumble. The time was just on two o'clock. The drive to Palma took an hour. At three, Dr Molina would undoubtedly be at home, where he would stay until the early evening. So to arrive at the clinic before six could only be to waste valuable time. He could enjoy his siesta with a happy conscience.

CHAPTER 4

Dr Molina was a small, precise, pedantically self-assured man who dressed with great care and spoke with the authority of someone who was unused to being contradicted. 'The señor arrived at the clinic during the night. I was called, since it was feared that his condition was serious enough to demand the highest skill, but my examination showed that his injuries were less than had at first been feared and were not life-threatening.'

'What sort of injuries were they?' Alvarez asked.

'Multiple, heavy bruising, burns, and a fractured arm. His condition now is comfortable.'

Doctors often spoke in a different language from their patients. Surely no man who had suffered serious bruising, a fractured arm, and burns, would describe his condition as comfortable? 'Is there something unusual about these injuries?'

'An extraordinary question, considering you are an inspector in the Cuerpo General de Policia and therefore might have been expected to have at least some knowledge of the facts!'

'I'm afraid I wasn't given any details by my superior chief. All I had was a phone call saying . . .'

'In my experience, excuses seldom excuse.'

There was a silence, then Alvarez said glumly: 'Perhaps you'd be kind enough to explain why you contacted the police?'

'Because it was my duty to do so. The bruising the señor suffered was probably caused by kicking; on his wrists and ankles were marks which, although very faint by the time I saw them, indicated that his limbs had been bound with thin cord; on his chest were burn marks caused by a lighted cigarette.'

'You're suggesting he was beaten up and tortured?'

'I am relating the facts, I leave you to draw the conclusions.'

'Have you asked him what happened?'

'Naturally, since I speak fluent English. He says he was up a stepladder, re-hanging a picture, and fell. At the time, he was smoking a cigarette and this was jerked out of his mouth to land on his chest. Because of the shock and growing pain in his arm and side, it was several seconds before he realized he was also being burned.'

'But that explanation seems unlikely to you?'

'Let me overlook the bruising and the marks of ligatures. The burns on his chest unmistakably formed a circle. Had he fallen and belatedly realized his chest was being burned, his first reaction must surely have been to sweep the cigarette off with his uninjured arm. Therefore, one would expect him to be burned either in one place only, or if in more than one then the burns to be in a rough line or a zigzag.'

'Have you any idea why he should lie about this?'

'No.'

'Could he be a masochist and his sadistic partner became over-enthusiastic?'

'My specialized knowledge does not lie in such objectionable fields,' replied Molina with distaste.

'Has he recovered sufficiently for me to question him?'

'He has.'

'Then I'll see if I can find out what really went on.'

Alvarez took a lift up to the fourth floor and walked along a corridor to Room 416. He knocked, went in. A very short passage, on the left of which was a bathroom, opened into a large, well-lit room which contained two beds, a settee, a chair, a chest of drawers, and a built-in cupboard. Through the window there was a view to the mountains which ran the length of the island, like a spine.

'Señor Franklin Gore? I wonder if you feel well enough to talk?'

'In English, more than well enough! My vocabulary of sign language ran out some time ago and the doctor, who claims it is English, is, I'm sure, really speaking Pashto.'

What a pity Molina could not have heard that! 'My name is Inspector Alvarez, of the Cuerpo General de Policia.'

'Sounds very official. Have a seat and tell me what brings a policeman here?'

Alvarez moved the chair closer to the right-hand bed on which Gore lay stripped to the waist, his chest bandaged and his left arm in plaster from the wrist to the elbow. 'I should like to ask a few questions concerning the cause of your injuries.'

'Presumably because of the doctor? The man's a pompous idiot.'

Alvarez warmed to the Englishman. 'I am afraid that I have to be guided by what he says.'

'So what exactly is that?'

'To begin with, that the bruises were probably caused by kicking.'

'I collected them when I fell off a stepladder. I read only the other day that more accidents occur in the home because of ladders than from any other appliance. Unwittingly, I've added to the statistics.'

'He also said that there were marks on your wrists and ankles which had been caused by thin cord being lashed around them.'

Gore laughed. 'As I tried to explain to him, the man who can climb a stepladder with both feet and hands tied should apply to the nearest circus.'

'And there are burns on your chest.'

'They, as a matter of fact, are stinging like hell. Have

you noticed how it's often the little injuries that cause the
most discomfort? My side and arm give me hell if I don't
move as carefully as if I were lying on a fakir's mat, but
otherwise I can ignore them; but the burns remind me of
their presence all the time.'

'I believe you were smoking when up the ladder?'

'I've promised myself with monotonous regularity that
I'll give up smoking; with an equally monotonous regularity
I've breached that promise. Do you smoke?'

'Regretfully, yes.'

'I've none, so if you were to offer me one, I'd remember
you in my will.'

Alvarez stood, brought a pack of cigarettes and a lighter
from his pocket. He offered a cigarette, flicked open the
lighter. Gore inhaled, immediately coughed violently. He
gasped as the sudden movement caused him to move his
injured arm. He stubbed out the cigarette. 'They say that
anæsthetics and smoking don't mix. I'm here to confirm.'
He coughed again, less violently, cradled his arm. 'Sorry
about that. For the foreseeable future, I'm a non-smoker.'

'Señor, Doctor Molina says there are several distinct
burns on your chest and these form a circle. Does that not
seem rather odd?'

'I don't see why it should.'

'You fell off the stepladder and landed on your back and
the cigarette was jerked from your mouth to land on your
chest. As soon as you were conscious it was burning you,
you must have tried to brush it off. Would you not, therefore, expect just one burn; or, if you failed to brush it off
cleanly, a rough line of burns? But not a circle.'

'At first I thought the world had imploded, then I decided it probably hadn't. My arm and side were stabbing,
but the pain on my chest seemed more urgent. Being dazed,
it took me time to realize what was happening, then I
reached up to brush the cigarette away. That was when I

discovered my left arm was broken. To prove that the quickest way of overcoming one injury is to suffer another that's worse, I forgot the cigarette as I squirmed around, trying to find out how to hold my left arm so that it didn't dig knives into me. It was quite a while before I got round to using my right arm to sweep the cigarette off myself. Obviously, in the meantime it had been dancing a reel.'

'Yet the burns form a circle.'

'Aren't reels circular?' He laughed, winced. 'Laughing's as dangerous as smoking.'

'Señor, are you certain you were not tied up by someone who then kicked you and burned you with a lighted cigarette?'

'Quite certain. Who in the hell is going to break in and do all that to me?'

'Perhaps he did not have to break in; perhaps he was invited in. And initially perhaps you were willing to be tied up?'

'Is that a polite way of asking if I was taking part in a little S/M which got out of hand?'

'Were you?'

'In my book, sex should mean pleasure, not pain.'

'I believe that a masochist gains pleasure from pain.'

'Each to his own, as any amorous porcupine knows.'

'Are you certain that all your injuries were the result of the accident and none of them was inflicted by another person?'

'I couldn't be more certain.'

'Señor, why were you rehanging a painting?'

'It had fallen earlier when I brushed it with my hand by mistake and the hook pulled out of the wall. Unluckily, neither the glass nor the painting suffered. If it were mine, it would receive the heigh-ho into the dustbin, but it's part of the furnishings of the house, which I rent. Of course, it may not be quite as bad as all that—I'm the first to admit

that when it comes to modern-style painting, I'm the original Philistine.'

'How did you get help after the accident?'

'I lay for a time, cursing all stepladders and fools who
lean too far out instead of getting down and moving the
ladders, then gritted my teeth, remembered Horatius who
would have laughed at a mere broken arm, and dragged
myself into the hall. I phoned the next-door neighbour.'

'Thank you, señor, for your kindness in answering my
questions.' Alvarez stood, said goodbye, left. As he walked
towards the lift, he pondered the fact that Gore seemed far
too pleasant, cheerful, and forthcoming, to be a man who
pursued the more arcane sexual practices.

It was not easy to rise when the temperature felt as if it
must already have soared up into the 40s . . .

'Enrique,' Dolores shouted from downstairs, 'if you don't
get up now, it'll be lunch-time.'

He climbed off the bed, crossed to the window, unclipped
the shutters and pushed them back. Visible above the roofs
of the village was Puig María, on top of which were the
buildings which had once been a hermitage but which now,
due to a lack of hermits, were looked after by elderly nuns.
By definition, no one called on a hermit to rise at the crack
of dawn . . .

Half an hour later, he arrived in his office, sat behind the
desk, and stared at the day's mail which a cabo had put on
it. His eyelids grew heavy. Heat made a man sleepy . . .

The telephone jerked him awake and the plum-voiced
secretary said the superior chief wanted to speak to him.
As he waited, he looked at his watch. Very nearly merienda
time. A coffee and a coñac at the Club Llueso . . .

'What the devil's happened to your report on the Englishman?' demanded Salas.

'I've tried twice to ring you, señor, but each time the line was engaged. I was about to try a third time when you rang me . . . I went to the clinica and spoke to Dr Molina and Señor Gore. Dr Molina is of the decided opinion that the señor's injuries were inflicted by a second person; the marks on his wrists and ankles mean he was tied up, the bruises that he was kicked, and the burns on his chest that he was tortured.

'In direct contradiction, Señor Gore denies that he was attacked and tortured. He states that he fell off a ladder while rehanging a picture and all his injuries were suffered as a consequence of that fall.'

'Is the doctor mistaken or is the Englishman lying?'

'If the señor is lying, the question has to be asked, why? Initially, it seemed that the only feasible answer could be that he is trying to conceal the fact that he willingly subjected himself to acts of sadism and these got out of hand. But having spoken to him, I judge him to be a pleasant, normal man and I find it difficult to cast him in so perverted a role. Yet if he was beaten and tortured against his will, why doesn't he admit this, not least in order to gain protection in the future?'

Alvarez paused, briefly to commend himself on the fluent efficiency with which he was making the report. 'Señor, when one is trying to decide which of two persons is telling the truth, I am certain the answer often lies in the character of the person concerned. I have described Señor Gore's. Dr Molina is a man of unusual self-confidence and very conscious of his position. He will come to a decision quickly and then be loath ever to change this. Much of his argument in favour of assault and torture rests on the fact that the burns form a circle and therefore could not have been inflicted accidentally. But that is a factual, not a medical conclusion, and every detective is taught that while the impossible happens only occasionally, the improbable occurs more frequently. Is it not feasible that the shock of the fall from the stepladder so confused Señor Gore that his irrational, unco-ordinated efforts to remove the pain from his chest caused the lighted cigarette to rotate before he managed to brush it off himself? In other words, that the señor suffered the accident exactly as he described it?'

'Perfectly feasible. Unless, that is, one has sufficient initiative to learn the facts and discovers that a man was knocked unconscious outside the Englishman's house.'

CHAPTER 5

Altobarí was a small village which nestled in a valley in the
mountains. From there, a pigeon might be able to fly to
Palma in no time, but a man on a mule took most of the
day to make his laborious way over and around the mountains and so in pre-tourist times the community had been
virtually self-sufficient. The soil was stony and hard to
work, but plentiful underground water, brought up by traditional waterwheels worked by mules, had meant that fruit
and vegetables could be grown, and pigs, chickens, and a
few cows be kept; forgotten generations—some said the
Moors—had terraced the lower slopes and on these olive
and almond trees had flourished; wild goats, fleet of foot,
could occasionally be trapped to provide a feast . . . A man
might have had to labour every working hour of every day,
his world might have been so limited that he knew little
about what was happening even ten kilometres away, his
life might never have been touched by outside beauty, but
that had always been the peasants' lot . . . And then the
tourists had started to arrive on the island in ever increasing
numbers and there had been money available to widen
and surface mule tracks and to build new roads and soon
Altobarí had ceased to be isolated. Mules had given way to
bicycles, bicycles to mopeds, mopeds to cars. The hundreds
of hotels built on the coast had needed staff and the young
had gone to work in them. As the older people died, or
could no longer work the fields, the least productive land
was abandoned, then even some of the more productive;
waterwheels went unrepaired and, where water was still
needed, were replaced with electric pumps; when the stone
walls of the terraces crumbled, they were no longer rebuilt

. . . Within a single generation, the character of the village and the lives of those who lived in it had changed. It took a clever man to know whether it was for the better or the worse.

Alvarez parked his car in the small square in front of the church and puffed his way along two narrow streets to the house where, he was told, Vicente Otero lived. He stepped through the bead curtain into a traditional room, dimly lit because the shutters were closed, furnished for formal occasions, and called out. A woman came through from the next room. He introduced himself, asked if Vicente was at home.

She was slightly older than he and could remember when a visit from authority—even a village as isolated as Altobarí had always been within their sights—could have dangerous consequences. She nervously moistened her lips, looked anywhere but at him.

'I just want to ask him a few questions about what happened Monday night.'

His quiet, friendly voice gave her a measure of confidence which showed itself in a rush of words. 'Vicente's my only son because the good Lord took my husband soon after he was born. Mother of God, the doctors told me it was a miracle he was not killed. If his skull had been no thicker than usual . . . Who could have been so vicious?'

'I am here to try and find out. Is he at home?'

'He's resting. The hospital wanted him to stay, but he said he must come home. He has terrible pains in his head. The doctor says they will go, but . . .' She stopped as imagined fears crowded her mind.

'Believe the doctor, señora. Now, if he's up to it, I'd like a word with him.'

She crossed to the window and opened the shutters, so that the harsh light streamed in, then left. He sat on a traditionally shaped wooden chair with rush seat and won-

dered if there was any chance of his returning home in time
for lunch? He thought he'd heard Dolores mention pollastre
farcit amb magrana. It made a man's mouth water even to
think about it . . .

Otero entered the room, followed by his mother. There
was no mistaking the relationship between them, any more
than it was possible to miss the fact that the lines of accept-
ance in her face had become lines of weakness in his. She
settled next to him and Alvarez was reminded of the old
adage: A thrush defending her young becomes an eagle.
'I want a chat about what happened Monday evening,' he
said.

'Why?' asked Otero sullenly. There was a large, square
patch of lint taped to the back of his head, which had been
shaved; he kept reaching up and touching it lightly with
his fingers.

'To find out exactly what happened, of course.'

'I was bloody near killed, that's what.'

She reached across to offer tactile consolation, but he
rejected her sympathy by brushing her hand away.

'Why should someone have attacked you?'

'How would I know?'

'Then we'll have to try and find out.'

'What's it matter?'

'You don't want the guilty person caught?'

'Of course I do. Only I didn't see nothing.'

'Where were you when you were hit?'

There was a silence.

'Tell the inspector,' said his mother.

'I was in the road, walking.'

'That's outside the house that's let to the Englishman,
Señor Gore?'

'Yeah.'

'What were you doing there?'

'Ain't I just said?'

'Vicente . . .' began his mother, worried by his sullen rudeness, then stopped.

'Where were you walking to?'

'Just walking.'

'I had a look at the señor's house before I came here. It's a good kilometre out of the village and the road doesn't lead anywhere. It seems an odd place to be walking at that time of night.'

'I've friends live further along.'

'You don't know anyone who lives along there, do you?' she asked, surprised.

'Why don't you shut up?'

'Señora,' said Alvarez, 'it will be better if you leave. Perhaps your son has things to tell me which are difficult to speak in front of a mother.'

'I've nothing to say,' Otero muttered.

'That is unfortunate.' Alvarez's tone was sharp, expressing his contempt for a son who could speak to his mother as the other had just done.

She made a whimpering sound as she came to her feet. 'I swear he's a good boy.'

'He has a good mother,' Alvarez said enigmatically. He watched her leave the room, then turned. 'So?'

'I was walking along the road and got hit. That's all.'

'The driver of the passing car found you collapsed across the stone wall which surrounds the señor's property. When he asked you what had happened, you mumbled that you'd been attacked in the garden and after recovering consciousness you'd tried to climb the wall, but hadn't the strength.'

'I never said that. The driver's lying.'

'A man doesn't lie unless he has reason to and he's none. So what's your reason? To try to hide the fact that you intended to break into the house?'

'I've never stolen in my life.'

'There's always a first time.'

'I swear I'm not a thief,' he said hoarsely.

'Then what were you doing in the garden?'

He didn't answer, looked longingly at the inner door.

'Are you fit enough to move?'

'Move where?'

'To Palma, so that you can be charged with attempting to commit burglary.'

Otero's lips trembled and he looked as if he might burst into tears. Alvarez waited with the endless patience which came naturally to a peasant.

Otero used a handkerchief to mop the sweat from his forehead. He fingered the lint on his head. He looked at Alvarez, then hurriedly away. He began to speak falteringly, swallowing words, his voice so low it was only just audible.

It had all started some time ago. Girls didn't seem to like him and since most of his male contemporaries worked away from home, were married, or had novias, most of his spare time had to be spent on his own. He'd fallen into the habit of wandering the mountains and by chance one day he'd started to descend the slope which backed the villa one of the foreigners lived in. The señor and a woman with blonde hair had been in the shallow end of the pool. Nothing extraordinary about that except that, being out of sight of the road or another house, they'd been enjoying themselves in a way not normally associated with swimming pools. He should have moved on, of course, respecting their privacy even if, being foreigners, they'd no sense of shame, but the pleasure of watching had been too great . . .

He'd gone back many times, without success, then one evening, as the sky had become tinged with mauve, she'd been back. He'd watched from a hiding-place. At first they'd just lounged in patio chairs, drinking. Only when it was too dark for him to be able to see them clearly had they gone inside. A light had gone on in one room. He'd naturally expected them to close the shutters, but they hadn't . . .

He'd seen the blonde a couple of times more, then she'd vanished. Her place had been taken by an older woman with raven black hair. She'd lacked fire. When they were in the pool, they swam; on the patio, they merely drank and chatted like married people; when they went into the house, the shutters were closed . . . Of course, if one bent down to look up between the slats of a shutter, one could see part of the room beyond, but since the line of sight was sharply upwards, those inside had to be close to the window to offer a rewarding view . . .

'On Monday night, then, you were in the garden, hoping to see what was happening inside the house?'

'I thought maybe the blonde was back.' He smirked as he looked across. It seemed that by admitting he was a voyeur he had not only lessened his own sense of shame, he imagined he had drawn Alvarez into his twisted world.

'Did you find out if she had returned?'

'I didn't find out anything. I hadn't got up to the house when I was knocked out.'

'Were the shutters open?'

'I . . . I think they were, but I'm not certain. It's all a bit hazy now.'

'Was there a car parked in the road or the drive?'

'I wouldn't know. I came up to the garden from the back.'

'Have you any idea who attacked you?'

'Of course I ain't. I didn't hear or see nothing. One moment I was walking towards the window through which I'd seen the blonde and him . . . The next, it was nothing until I regained consciousness and felt as if my head had been split wide open. The doctor said that if I didn't have an unusually thick skull, I'd be dead. As it is, I get headaches what make me wish I were.'

Gore might have discovered that he was being watched by a Peeping Tom and had determined to discourage the pest, but the assault had been so vicious. Gore seemed genial, pleasant, good-humoured, and such men didn't act like that even when provoked.

'What are you going to do?' demanded Otero.

'Think about it,' replied Alvarez.

CHAPTER 6

A detective learned many useful knacks, one of which was how to force the average house lock in ten seconds flat. Alvarez should, of course, have requested Gore's permission to enter the house or have obtained a court order entitling him to do so, but the proper channels always meant delay. He was about to insert the first of seven skeleton keys into the lock when the door was pulled open. 'What do you want?' demanded a woman aggressively.

Overcoming his surprise, he said defensively: 'I didn't expect anyone to be here.' Hastily, he pocketed the keys.

'That's obvious.'

'Cuerpo General de Policia.'

'Prove it.'

He searched his pockets for his identifying warrant. 'I'm afraid I haven't got it on me . . .'

'Then you don't come in.' She slammed the door shut and he heard the snap of the lock.

He made his way back and was almost at the wrought-iron gates, typically of such elaborate design they might have been guarding a mansion, when his memory dredged up the shadowy picture of his putting the warrant in the glove locker. Yet why on earth should he have done that? . . . It was there. He returned to the door, rang the bell. She opened the door and studied the warrant intently.

'What's your name?'

'Aguenda Sitzar, if it's any concern of yours.' Unlike Otero's mother, she had no memories of the time when only a fool spoke to a policeman as she had just done.

'You do the housework here?'

'And cook, if he wants.' Her features matched her

manner—solidly pugnacious. If she had known the bloom of youth, it had early deserted her.

'You must know that the señor was attacked and injured and is in a clinic in Palma?'

'Of course,' she replied scornfully. In a village the size of Altobarí, little was confidential.

'I saw him earlier on and he's cheerful, despite everything. He seems to be a nice chap.'

'For a foreigner.'

'I was puzzled about how he came to be injured. He couldn't really tell me—still confused by the shock, I suppose.'

'He fell off a stepladder. Like Jorge did last year, only Jorge smashed his hip and hasn't walked since.'

'Where did the señor do that?'

'In the sitting-room.'

'I'd like to have a look.'

She hesitated, then led the way into an L-shaped area in which the dining-room was separated from the sitting-room by a wide, open archway.

'It looks like you've tidied things up.'

'D'you think I'm paid to sit on my arse?' Throughout the island, the women of Altobarí were condemned for their crude tongues.

'So where did you put the stepladder?'

'What are you on about?'

'The ladder he fell off.'

'That's where it's always kept, in the garage.'

'And you put it there?'

'Haven't touched it.'

'Then I guess the Englishman who came to the señor's help must have returned it.'

She shrugged her shoulders.

'Tell me something. Were there a lot of cigarette stubs lying about the place?'

''Course not.'

'Why of course?'

She replied that the señor didn't smoke and why was he wasting her time by asking a load of ridiculous questions? Alvarez used a handkerchief to wipe away the sweat—with neither a fan nor the air-conditioning unit switched on, the room was like an oven. In the hospital, Gore had made a point of asking for a cigarette, proving he was a confirmed smoker. No wonder he'd coughed and stubbed out the cigarette almost immediately. 'Was this room in a hell of a mess when you arrived Monday morning?'

'No more than usual.'

'So what exactly was it like?'

She said, with undiminished antagonism: 'There was newspapers on the floor, a shirt lying around, that sort of thing.'

'What was the shirt doing in here?'

'Why ask me?'

'What did you do with it?'

'Mended it, then washed it with the other things in the machine.'·

'What needed mending?'

'Two buttons had been pulled off so I sewed 'em back on.'

'Did he often leave clothes lying about the place?'

'It's not the first time, only previously they weren't his.'

'How can you be certain?'

'Because he doesn't wear scraps of lace that would make any decent woman blush just to think about 'em.'

'So who had worn them?'

'That woman with blonde hair.'

'What d'you know about her?'

'Only that whenever she spent all night here, she didn't disturb a bed in one of the other rooms so as I could think she'd slept in that.'

'Obviously a woman without much sense of shame.'

'Didn't know the meaning of the word. I came back one afternoon to give the señor something and there she was, lying by the pool without even a costume on. Think about that!'

He tried not to. 'Is she a foreigner?'

'You imagine any Mallorquin could behave like that?'

She was not being naïve, as would have been the case had she lived on the coast. Those who lived in the inland villages and had limited contact with foreigners had managed to retain the old values. 'Have you any idea where she is now?'

'Of course I don't.' She could hardly have been more indignant if he'd asked her to name the nearest whorehouse.

'Recently, the señor's been friendly with another woman; older and with very black hair. What's she like?'

Aguenda enjoyed a gossip, when the subject was not a slut about whom a decent woman could admit to knowing nothing. Señora Vivien was a nice, friendly woman. Both she and the señor were stupid, of course, calling her señorita. Didn't they have the sense to realize that the narrow band of white on the third finger of her left hand marked her as clearly as if she'd left the wedding ring on? . . . No, she didn't know what the señora's surname was. How did one ever know a foreigner's surname since it seemed to be their extraordinary custom to have only one and not, as in a civilized country, two? She was English; or at least she and the señor always spoke to each other in English. And from something the señor had once said she lived near Llueso. Rich like all foreigners. Drove a truly enormous red car. Diego said that it was a Mercedes and cost fifteen million pesetas. Diego was a liar and no car could cost that much, nevertheless . . . As far as she knew, the señora had never spent a whole night at the villa . . .

There was only one framed painting in the room and he

crossed to study it, then reached up to lift it off its hook. When the wall had last been decorated, the hook had been in place and there was paint on it; that paint was unbroken, making it clear that the hook had not recently been moved. He replaced the painting. That he could do so without steps meant that Gore, who stood several centimetres taller, would not have needed a stepladder.

'What's all this about?' she demanded for a second time.

'I have to try and find out why Vicente Otero was attacked. Have you any idea what he was doing in the garden that night?'

'No.'

Her tone told him all that her monosyllabic reply had not. She had a very good idea, but would never expose Otero's shame to a man who was not only a detective, but more importantly, not a local.

'Then you can't make a guess at who might have attacked him?'

'Can't I?'

'Can you?'

'It was the gipsy couple. Been in the village, trying to sell things. I told 'em when they came to my house, if you're not gone by the time I get my husband, you'll not be in a fit state to go thieving anywhere else . . .'

He listened, saddened that here was part of the past which had not changed. From time immemorial, gipsies had been hated and feared. If one refused them alms, they cast spells which dried up cows, sickened goats, even struck down humans. Many had become too sophisticated to believe in such rubbish, but even they condemned as guilty any gipsies who were present in the area in which petty crime took place.

'I doubt we need worry about them.'

She did not try to hide her contempt for his stupidity.

*

The next villa was over half a kilometre along the road. Smaller than the one he had just left, the garden was a mass of colour, making it obvious that at least one of the occupants was an enthusiastic gardener.

An elderly woman, with white, wavy hair, opened the door and asked him in tortured Spanish what he wanted. He replied, in English, that he'd be grateful for a word with her and the señor, were the latter at home. She led the way through the house to the patio where, sitting in the shade of bamboo mats laid on top of a wire frame, was her husband.

'You've come because of what happened to poor old Franklin?' Eric Wilson spoke loudly.

'Indeed, señor. But there is also the problem of who knocked Otero unconscious in the señor's garden and why.'

'No need to wonder why. Because he's a Peeping Tom, that's why.'

'You mustn't say that,' protested his wife. She looked uneasily at Alvarez. 'I know that's what Rosa told us, but one shouldn't believe everything she says. Especially when ... Not when you're talking to ...' She came to a stumbling stop and sought a way out of her embarrassment. 'Inspector, please sit down and would you like to join us in a drink?'

Alvarez said he'd very much like a brandy.

She collected her husband's empty glass from the table, left her own. As she went into the house, Alvarez sat on one of the uncomfortable metal chairs. 'Perhaps you will tell me what happened Sunday night, señor?'

'It's quickly told. We were in bed and had just turned the lights off when the phone rang. I said to Monica, who the hell's ringing this late? Turned out to be Franklin, shouting for help. I put on some clothes and went along. I'll be perfectly frank. When I first saw him, I felt queasy.'

'Why was that?'

'Why? Because he was in such a mess, that's why. I'm

not a man for violence. Turn the films off if they're violent.'

'Did he look as if he'd been attacked?'

His wife returned to the patio, a tray in her hand. She passed one glass to Alvarez, the other to her husband, sat.

Wilson drank eagerly. He jerked his head in the direction of Alvarez. 'He's asking if Franklin looked as if he'd been attacked. Maybe he doesn't understand what he's saying.'

Her expression became even more worried than before. She stared at her husband, willing him to start showing common sense and tact.

'Where exactly was the señor when you arrived in the house?'

'Lying on the floor, not far from the settee, and looking like he was about to peg out. His face was the colour of parchment. I can tell you, I was on to the phone in a bloody hurry to tell the lady wife to call for help. I couldn't do that myself because I don't speak the lingo.'

'Did you move the stepladder back into the garage?'

'What stepladder?'

'The one that was lying on the floor close to Señor Gore.'

'There wasn't one. You've got it all wrong. Which on this island is par for the course.'

'Eric!' she expostulated. 'You mustn't say that sort of thing.'

'I reckon the Inspector knows as well as me that if there are two ways of doing something, the locals will always choose the wrong one.'

Not for the first time, Alvarez was astonished at the ability of some Englishmen to be insulting without ever realizing the fact. 'Was the señor wearing a shirt?'

'You ask some weird questions, no argument! No, he wasn't, but I'll be shot if I can see what that has to do with anything.'

'Probably nothing, but I have discovered that it is always

best to try to find out everything in the hopes that something will be of use.'

'Then maybe you'd like to know what we had for supper before we went to bed that night?' He chuckled at his own wit.

'Please, Eric,' she pleaded.

'Señor,' Alvarez asked, 'have you any idea who assaulted Otero?'

'Didn't you know my middle name's Sherlock? It was that gippo, that's who.'

Alvarez was gratified to discover that a sophisticated Englishman could be as blindly and stupidly prejudiced as a simple Mallorquin villager.

CHAPTER 7

Even were he to drive like Jehu, he could not hope to return home in time for lunch. Earlier, he'd noticed a cellar in the village and so he decided to eat there; since few foreigners would frequent it, it would serve honest food at not too dishonest prices.

He sat at one of the tables which were set between two rows of enormous wooden barrels in which wine had once been kept and ordered frito Mallorquin. But even as he ate that, and accepted that it was good, he lamented the fact he was not enjoying pollestre farcit amb magrana, that heavenly concoction of thin slices of chicken seasoned with onion, pomegranate seeds, pork, egg, milk, white wine, breadcrumbs, lard, nutmeg, pepper, salt, and pomegranate sauce . . .

He drove south from Altobarí—initially, because of the lie of the mountains, having to travel west instead of east —and thought about what he'd learned. It seemed clear that Gore was lying. Why was he insisting that he'd suffered an accident when the briefest of inquiries showed that he had not—because it had not occurred to him that there would be an inquiry? His false denial that he'd been beaten up and tortured meant that he didn't wish the motives for his injuries or the identity of his torturer, or both, to be made public. A jealous husband? A womanizer such as he might have given any number of husbands cause to be jealous . . .

He arrived home just after four. He went upstairs to lie down because he'd had a very busy day.

*

He climbed the stairs to his office, waited until he'd regained his breath, then phoned Traffic in Palma. 'Will you check out the owner of a car for me? It's a Mercedes, new or nearly new.'

'What model?'

'I don't know.'

'What colour?'

'I don't know that either.'

'Are you sure it's got four wheels?'

'The owner's a foreigner, perhaps a woman whose Christian name is Vivien; she probably lives this end of the island.'

'You make my job too easy,' said the other bad-temperedly, before ringing off.

Alvarez leaned back in the chair, lit a cigarette, and thought that life wasn't all anguish. Dolores had cooked sopa torrada for the lunch he'd missed. The pollastre was for supper . . .

He suddenly remembered something, rang Traffic a second time. 'That Mercedes is red.'

Thursday was, incredibly, even hotter than Wednesday had been. To walk from shade into sunshine was to enter a furnace. So many air-conditioning units were turned to maximum, so many fans to full speed, that demand out-stripped supply and the electricity was cut; water was turned off in Llueso and all available supplies were chan-nelled down to the port so that the tourists, who knew little about the economical use of water, could be free to waste it; wells which never dried out, dried out; the leaves of citrus trees curled as they lessened the area they presented the burning sun . . .

Sweat trickled down Alvarez's cheeks on to his chin and then fell, landing on the pencilled notes he'd just made. He mopped his face and neck. Sweet Mary, but a man was not intended to work in such a heat . . . He tried to concentrate on what he'd written. Five people who lived in the area had bought red Mercedes that year and twelve the previous; of these, nine were foreigners . . . How had eight locals found the money to buy such cars when the socialist government was forever raising taxes? He realized he was being naïve because of the heat. Madrid might promulgate a dozen new taxes, but they'd never convince a single Mallorquin that taxation was other than voluntary . . . He rang the foreign department of the internal ministry. Had any of the following names a wife called Vivien?

The reply was satisfactory. Sir Donald Macadie, Bart did. He asked for, and was given, their address.

He settled back in the chair and lit a cigarette. An English woman had once tried to explain to him the British system of titles, but he'd become lost when she'd said that a husband's name could be different from his wife's, both could be different from their elder son's, and all three could be different from their younger son's. Still, one thing was clear, a title meant Sir Bart was a man of wealth and authority and such men did not take lightly to their wives' infidelities. As the old Mallorquin saying put it: Pinch a lamb and it bleats; pinch a bull and it charges.

He parked, climbed out of the car and looked around. It was almost certainly the most dramatic site he'd ever seen. Then æsthetic pleasure gave way to practical considerations. The land beyond the garden was rock and only small, stunted clumps of grass and weeds grew in crevices which meant that the construction of a garden rich enough to support flowerbeds, lawn, and trees must have needed a staggering amount of soil; the water to maintain this garden must call for countless truckloads at a cost that staggered . . .

Faced with the choice of three houses, he chose the

middle and largest. He rang the bell by the side of the front door and waited, watching as he did so an Eleonara's Falcon scythe effortlessly overhead.

The door was opened by a young woman, ripely attractive, dressed in a crisply neat, blue maid's dress. He introduced himself, asked if Sir Bart were at home.

'Who?'

He gave the full name.

She giggled.

Giggling females disturbed him, making him feel older than he wished. 'This is not a laughing matter,' he said in his most authoritative voice.

'Don't you know?' she asked pertly, clearly unworried by his manner. 'The señor's name is Sir Donald Macadie. Bart is a bit extra which he sticks on; don't ask me why.'

The woman who had tried to teach him about British titles had not got this far. 'Never mind all that, is he in?'

'No.'

'Then is his wife?'

'They're both in Rome. The señora said she wasn't feeling too good, so they flew there Wednesday to try to cheer her up.'

'How long are they gone for?'

She shrugged her shoulders. 'With them, there's no knowing.'

Routine was for the little people of the world. 'So who's here now?'

'There's only me and Eloisa. Ana and Mauricio are on holiday for a week.'

A very light breeze ruffled his hair and for the first time he stopped to realize that the heat was slightly less than stifling up here; were there no bounds to what wealth could provide? 'Then I'd like a word with the two of you.'

She fidgeted with a button on her dress. 'Well, it's like this . . .' She trailed off into silence.

'When the farmer's in bed, the hedgehog suckles the cow?'

'What's that supposed to mean?'

'That maybe Eloisa's taking a little time off since the bosses are away?'

'We've cleaned everywhere and polished all the furniture. And I'm here for the phone or if anyone turns up.'

'Since I'm not paying the bills . . . Then it's going to be just you and me for a chat.'

'What's up? I don't know anything about anything.'

He smiled, momentarily banishing his normally lugubrious expression. 'A sweeping denial! There's no cause to worry, it's just that you may be able to help me.' Something about her had been puzzling him and now he said: 'You seem to remind me of someone.'

'Who?'

'Marta Nicolau.'

'Then that's not surprising since she's my aunt.'

'And you're Mercedes's daughter, Enriqueta. I'm Dolores Raméz's cousin; only really it's a lot more distant relationship than first cousin.'

She lost any sense of unease. She suggested they went through to the patio and did he fancy a drink? As he sat in the shade of a patio umbrella, stared out across the elaborately shaped swimming-pool at the distant Llueso Bay, and drank a brandy of a quality superior to Carlos I, he decided that it would not be difficult to accustom himself to the life of a millionaire.

He asked her what her employers were like—typical rich foreigners who thought they'd bought the people whose wages they paid? She was indignant. The señor and señora were nothing like that. They were grand people, all right —more millions of pesetas than there were stars in the sky —but they were still friendly and thoughtful. The señora expected things to be done correctly, but she was quick to praise; the señor was full of laughter, especially when he tried to speak Spanish, and generous. When Ana's uncle had died, he'd bought tickets for both her and Mauricio to fly to the funeral . . .

She saw that he'd finished his drink and asked him if he'd like another? When she had fetched it for him and was once more settled at the table, he said: 'How d'you reckon the señor and señora get on together?'

The señor was very restrained, never showing overt affection, but then everyone knew that Englishmen only made a fuss of their dogs. But one merely had to see the way he looked at her, opened doors for her, came to his feet when she entered the room, to know how fond of her he was. And that brooch he'd given her on her last birthday! A man had really to adore his wife to buy her jewellery like that . . .

'And she's as fond of him as he is of her?'

For the first time, she hesitated. When she spoke, it was as if each word had to be weighed. The señora went to a lot of trouble to make certain the señor had a pleasant life; she fussed over him and when he'd had a bit of pain in his chest, she'd insisted they immediately drove into Palma to see a specialist, even though he'd repeatedly said that it was all over and done with; and yet . . .

She dipped her forefinger into the white wine she was drinking, ran it round the rim of the glass to raise a screeching note. 'It's not so long ago she told him she thought it would be best if they had separate bedrooms.' She removed her hand.

'I've read that in England the rich often have separate bedrooms so as they can keep all their energies for fox-hunting.'

She giggled, then said: 'I bet he doesn't snore as much as she says he does.' She looked quickly at him, to see if he was going to speak. When he didn't, she once more ran her finger round the rim of the glass. 'At school, I learned

English. It was so difficult because nothing's spoken like it's written and my mum made me have extra lessons. I still can't really talk it, but I understand quite well and only the other day when the señor had driven off to the village . . . I shouldn't be telling you this.'

'I'm like a priest.'

'You mean you prefer foxhunting too?' she said pertly.

He smiled. 'I mean that what's told to me is told in complete confidence.'

'Well, I was dusting upstairs and I guess the señora didn't know I was because she was talking on the telephone and the door of her bedroom wasn't properly shut. She sounded almost hysterical, saying over and over again— her Spanish sounds funny—that she had to speak to someone who was in the hospital. First, I thought it was the señor who'd had an accident, but then she spoke a name.'

'Which was?'

'I don't remember, but it wasn't the señor's.'

'Franklin Gore?'

'It could've been.'

'Did she speak to him?'

'In the end. And she was real frantic, wanting to know if he was all right and not seriously ill.'

'So they're pretty good friends?'

'They're not just friends from the state she was in!'

'Were you surprised?'

'I was. And then again, I wasn't.' She drank, put the glass down on the table. 'Some time ago, she started aerobics classes on account of needing to keep fit. She bought all the gear and went into Palma two or three times a week . . . The funny thing was, when she got back she put her clothes out for washing and although the leotard was crumpled, it never looked like it had really been worn and nor did the underwear. I mean, in this sort of weather one sweats and sweats. It was Ana who first said that maybe . . .' She giggled. 'Eloisa says Ana's so sharp on account of having to watch Mauricio.'

'Would you think the señor worried about the trips to Palma?'

'If he did, there wasn't any sign of it. He always treats her like I wish someone would treat me.'

'It'll happen,' he said, with flattering certainty. 'So even before you overheard the telephone call to the hospital, you'd begun to think that maybe she had a boyfriend?'

'Well, sort of.'

'Have you any idea who he could be?'

'There's no saying. I mean, there's never been anyone here who she's looked at in that kind of way.'

'Is she the same age as her husband?'

'Nothing like.'

'So how old d'you reckon they both are?'

It was difficult to judge the señora's age. Women such as she spent their lives in luxury and fed their skins with nostrums which cost fortunes. But if one looked closely, there were lines about her eyes, the skin on her neck wasn't as taut as it might be, she needed to wear elastic pants, but didn't, and there was a lot of spare flesh around her thighs. She'd never see thirty again. And the señor was an old man —well over sixty.

He was about to tell her that sixty was far from old, but checked the words. He drained his glass.

'D'you fell like another?'

As she left, he thought that here was a triangle which had been known long before Euclid. A husband much older than his wife and no longer able to supply the excitement that a younger man was only too willing to offer . . .

He felt his left arm begin to burn because of the shifting shade and moved his chair. It was not difficult to envisage the sequence of events. The señora had rung Ca'n Renato, Aguenda had told her that Gore was in hospital and, being

Mallorquin, had exaggerated the injuries until she had made it seem that his last breath would be released at any moment. Frantic, the señora had rung the clinic. When she'd learned that he was not as badly injured as she'd believed, her relief had been so great that she had been deprived of both caution and common sense. She'd said she was rushing in to see him. He, emotion tempered by pain, had warned her not to be so rash. A clinic was a public place and they had mutual friends; what if she were seen there? Or if one of the nurses came from Llueso? Or if one of the doctors had met her socially? . . . Passion, as distinct from love, flourished on frustration. She'd had to persuade her husband to take her away to Rome so that she would know that the man she desired was out of reach . . .

Enriqueta returned and handed him the refilled glass. 'You look like something's upset you.'

'Only the thought that it can be a sad world.' He drank. 'D'you think you could find me a photo of the señora? It need only be a snapshot. I'll have it back to you within a couple of days.'

CHAPTER 8

Aguenda opened the front door of Ca'n Renato. 'Caught the gipsy, have you, what near killed Vicente?' she asked belligerently.

'Still checking,' Alvarez answered. 'Would you know if any of the locals saw the gipsy near here on Sunday night?'

'What's that matter?'

'If he wasn't seen in the vicinity at around the time of the assault, and Otero didn't see who hit him, what's to prove the gipsy had anything to do with it?'

'Because he did, that's why.'

Logic never overcame prejudice. 'I'd like you to do something for me.'

'What?' she demanded, as if she feared his intentions.

He showed her the photograph which Enriqueta had given him the previous day. 'D'you recognize this person?'

She studied the photo, eyes slightly screwed up because she should have worn glasses. 'That's her.'

'Who do you mean?'

'Who d'you think I mean? The woman the señor's been seeing. Not the blonde puta, the nice one with black hair.'

He drove into the underground car park, then climbed the stairs to the Plaza Major. After crossing to the north side of the square, a five-minute walk brought him to Calle General de Vega (altered, but not obscured, with a spray can to Carrer Urra).

The studio of Sanidad y Eficiencia was on the second floor of a five-storey building. On the television, aerobics classes were filled with young ladies, every one of whom was long-legged and lithesome; one quick glance told

Alvarez that none of the seven women in the class in progress was young, long-legged, or lithesome.

The owner of the studio had a pleasant manner, but
the sharp expression in her eyes suggested she was a keen
businesswoman. 'What exactly is it you want, Inspector?'

'A word about one of your clients.'

'The relationship is a confidential one.'

'Of course. And since the matter with which I am concerned is equally or even more confidential, we can both be
satisfied that nothing that's said will go beyond the office.'

She disliked authority, but reluctantly accepted that in
many circumstances she had to work with it because she
had to have a licence to run the business and building
regulations were so chaotic, often even unintelligible, that
it would not be difficult to find her in breach of them.

'Lady Macadie. Does she come here regularly?'

'Why d'you want to know?'

'Because she may inadvertently be involved in a case I'm
investigating. There's nothing criminal about what she's
done, it's just that she may be friendly with someone who's
been injured and I'm trying to identify the assailant. Her
friendship may be important, even though she doesn't
realize that.'

'You seem to be very uncertain. Surely, the simplest thing
is to ask her your questions, not me?'

'She's in Rome.'

She picked up a pencil and fiddled with it. He waited,
with the stolid patience which could be so disturbing
because it was clearly never-ending.

She put the pencil down, having made up her mind, and
spoke briskly. 'When the señora first came here she asked
me when the classes were held and whether we offered
individual tuition. I tried to explain that individual tuition
really defeated the object, but she said she preferred it and
was prepared to pay, within reason, whatever I cared to

ask. If I advise a client what is in her best interests and she chooses to ignore me . . .' She shrugged her shoulders. 'I named a fee. She then said that if she arranged a time, but didn't turn up, she'd pay double if I'd tell anyone who called or phoned and asked for her that she'd just completed her lesson and left to do some shopping.'

'Did you agree to that?'

'It's not up to me to sit in judgement.'

'You're presuming she was having an affair?'

'Of course.'

'Did she ever attend a class?'

'Once. Presumably to learn what happened so as to be able to provide an authentic background if questioned.'

There seemed to be no limit to the perfidy of which a woman was capable.

He drove into the car park of Clinica Barón, walked across to the main entrance, took the lift to the fourth floor and Room 416. Gore sat by the window, listening to the BBC World Service on a small radio. He switched that off.

'Good morning, señor. How are you now?'

'Returning to normal and hoping to be out of here very soon . . . A friend has brought me a few necessities of life so I can offer you sweet red Martini, brandy, or Scotch. And since there's a charming young nurse who speaks adequate English who's just started, I'm also supplied with ice.'

'Then I would like a coñac with ice only, please.' He saw that Gore was about to move. 'Can I get it to save you?'

'Thanks, but it does me good to move around, even if, as always, having good done to one has its painful moments . . . Grab a seat while I set things up.' Gore went over to the chest of drawers on which were bottles, a Thermos flask, and glasses, poured out two drinks. He handed Alvarez one glass, returned to his chair. 'So now that the important things in life have been dealt with, tell me what's brought you back here?'

'I need to ask you some more questions.'

'Questions come easily, answers can be more difficult. Still, fire away and I'll help if I can.'

'Was your assailant Sir Donald Macadie?'

Gore took his time drinking. He rested the glass on the arm of his chair. 'You surprise me! I mean this as no criticism, but I'd have said you were too down-to-earth to ask a question that far-fetched.'

'But you know him and someone had reason to attack and torture you.'

'You surely haven't decided to believe that fatuous doctor after all?'

'I visited your villa and spoke to Aguenda.'

'Then I hope the conversation was more scintillating than those I have with her. But then, of course, she can't pretend not to understand you.'

'You told me you were burned because you were smoking when you were on the ladder. She says you do not smoke.'

'Which proves that while no man is a hero to his valet, he is a mystery to his daily. I certainly am not a regular smoker, but I do have the occasional cigarette when life gets too trying, which it does whenever I have to do something practical with my hands. I'm the kind of fumble-fisted for whom nails invariably bend, screw heads become burred, and wood splits.'

'I examined the hook on which the painting hangs and it did not pull out of the wall. I asked Aguenda whether she moved the stepladder after the accident and she says it was not in the sitting-room; I asked Señor Wilson if he'd returned it to the garage and he said not.'

'Which shows that in moments of stress or drama, people's memories go haywire. I've no idea who did move

it, but obviously someone did and I'd guess that that someone was Aguenda.'

'She told me about the ladies you have entertained.'

'A gross breach of confidence.'

'She mentioned a señora who drives a large red Mercedes. Sir Donald Macadie owns a nearly new red Mercedes. I have spoken to one of the maids who works for him
and she says the señora often goes to aerobics classes in
Palma; the owner of the studio says the señora has only
ever attended one. I showed Aguenda a photograph of Lady
Macadie and she identified the señora as someone who
visited your villa several times.'

Gore went to scratch his forearm and only then remembered that it was encased in plaster. 'A tickle one
can't reach is a worse torture than the Chinese dripping
tap.'

'Do you deny that Lady Macadie visited you many
times?'

'I would if I thought there was still any point in doing
so. As things are, however, there isn't and I don't.'

'And it was Sir Donald Macadie who, having learned
about the affair, assaulted you?'

'Do husbands still feel so aggrieved they assault the man
responsible for their wives' dishonour? That certainly
would maintain a link, however tenuous, with the days of
chivalry. But I'm afraid that in this case the facts are far
more prosaic and the noble Sir Donald did not don his
armour.'

'I regret that I think you are lying, señor.'

'It's every man's right to think what he will. But mull
over this, Inspector. If, because I have been bonking his
wife, I have suffered a thrashing at the hands of the
aggrieved husband, it would be rough justice. Then to name
him would not only be to deny him the equity of justice, it
would also be to deny myself the relief of absolution. So let

me make it quite clear, no one assaulted me and no matter
what the facts appear to suggest, my injuries were sustained
in an accident. Since without my evidence you can prove
nothing, I suggest that that is an end to everything.'

'I'm afraid not, since Vicente Otero was also assaulted
that night.'

'Should the name mean something to me?'

'He's from the village and was attacked in your garden,
probably a very short time before you received your injuries.'

Gore was silent for several seconds, then he said: 'Is that
on the level?' His tone had sharpened and he no longer
spoke facetiously.

'You didn't know about this?'

'How could I, stuck here in hospital?'

'Perhaps because it's reasonable to suppose that it was
you who attacked him.'

'Reasonable? Bloody absurd. Why the hell should I have
gone for someone I don't know?'

'He's a Peeping Tom.'

'Are you suggesting he was trying to peep on me?'

'He had been for several months; at times, with considerable success.'

Gore swore briefly, but violently. 'He should be locked
up.'

'Or taught a lesson with an iron bar?'

'You can forget that since I'd no idea he was creeping
around after cheap thrills.'

'If it was not you, it had to be Sir Donald Macadie. He
intended to teach you a lesson, but clearly would have
wanted to do so without any fear of compromising his wife
and exposing her shame to the world. He would have
intended merely to disable Otero, not place his life at risk,
but a man totally unused to violence has little idea of how
dangerous even a moderate blow can be . . . Having dis-

abled Otero, he entered your house satisfied he was safe from observation.'

'Earlier, I called you down-to-earth. I take that back and bury it. You don't have to play second fiddle to the great Munchausen.'

'Let me repeat this, señor. If it wasn't he who assaulted Otero, it had to be you.'

Gore said nothing. Alvarez drained his glass. 'Whatever the consequences, I assure you that in the long run it is always better to tell the truth.'

'And you also believe in fairies?'

He sighed, stood. It was always sad to see a man digging a deeper and deeper pit for himself, even if it was his own lust which had led to the first spit being removed.

Alvarez stared at the telephone on his desk. It was Saturday and almost lunch-time. He was meant to work through Saturday, as if the director general could decree that the weekend consisted solely of Sunday, but rumour suggested the superior chief had taken up golf and spent all Saturdays and Sundays on one of the island's courses, working himself into an ever greater fury. There was, then, small point in submitting a report before Monday.

He checked the time. It was still half an hour before his official lunch-hour began, but it had been a very tiring morning . . .

CHAPTER 9

When Alvarez telephoned at ten-thirty on Monday morning, the plum-voiced secretary said the superior chief was in his office and undoubtedly would wish to speak to him. The words had an ominous ring.

'I suppose I should be gratified that you've finally managed to find the time to report.'

It sounded as if the superior chief had sliced every ball he'd struck. 'Señor, investigations have taken rather a long time because the case has proved to be more complicated than it appeared. However, up to a point the truth is now clear. On the other hand, unfortunately there are still ambiguities.

'Basically, there are two cases. The first concerns Sir Donald Macadie who is married to a woman considerably younger than himself who has had an affair with Señor Gore; Sir Donald Macadie discovered this and determined either to seek revenge or to scare off Señor Gore and assaulted him. Señor Gore now refuses to admit he was attacked and lacking his evidence it seems doubtful anything more can be done.'

'In such circumstances, can anyone think there is cause for action?'

'Señor Gore was quite badly injured.'

'The world would have become a contemptible place if a wronged husband were not permitted to teach his wife's lover a painful lesson. Presumably, he has thrown her out of his house?'

'He's taken her to Rome for a holiday.'

'English husbands have no cojones,' said Salas scornfully.

'The second case concerns Otero. It seems he was a Peeping Tom.'

'Why is it, Alvarez, that you have only to become concerned with a case for it to become sordid?'

'I really don't think I can be blamed for that, señor . . . He was attacked, presumably, a little before Señor Gore was himself assaulted. Obviously, either Señor Gore was the assailant before he was in turn assaulted by Sir Donald Macadie, or Sir Donald Macadie was guilty. Unfortunately, the evidence is insufficient to identify which of the two it was.'

'That's interesting. It's interesting because it raises the question of why you have spent the entire weekend trying, and failing, to solve a crime that has already been solved?'

'I . . . I don't understand.'

'Hardly unusual. Otero's assailant was arrested on Saturday by Inspector Fiol.'

'But Señor Gore is in hospital and Sir Donald Macadie is in Rome.'

'He arrested a gipsy who's been hanging around the village causing trouble. Inspector Fiol is a man who sees merit in the obvious. Were I not a realist, I'd suggest you follow his excellent example.' He cut the connection.

Alvarez replaced the receiver. What possible motive could the gipsy have for the assault? And since Gore had as good as admitted that his assailant was Sir Donald Macadie, this was to accept without demur the coincidence of two distinct crimes being committed at the same place, and virtually the same time, by two different persons. (Of course, the suggestion he'd just made to Salas—that Gore might have been the assailant—had seemed to postulate that possibility, but in fact there was a definite connection between the two crimes.)

Inspector Fiol. The name began to ring a bell. There had been a drive to find entrants into the Cuerpo General de

Policia who had better academic qualifications and men with degrees had been excused the entrance exams; that was how Fiol had joined. It was rumoured that he was already marked for promotion to Comisario . . .

He checked the number, telephoned the police station of the Policia Armada y de Trafico from which Fiol worked. 'It's Enrique Alvarez, from Llueso. How are things with you?'

The pleasant introduction was spurned. 'Well?'

'I wonder if you'd tell me something? I've been in your area, investigating an assault on Señor Gore which Dr Molina reported . . .'

'I am well aware of the facts. And I think I should make it clear that I have informed the superior chief that there was absolutely no need for another officer to come butting into my territory.'

'I was asked to help because I speak English . . .'

'What is it you want to know?'

Another Madrileño? 'It's to do with a man I believe you've arrested for the assault on Vicente Otero.'

'You are referring to José Flores?'

'If that's his name. As I've just said—and you knew anyway—I've been looking into Señor Gore's case and I've become pretty certain there's a definite connection between that and Otero's assault and—'

'There is no connection.'

'It isn't asking for a pretty heavy coincidence if there isn't? You know, it's my experience . . .'

'I concern myself with facts, not experiences. Flores and the woman had been making a nuisance of themselves for several days. When I questioned him, I found him to be in possession of a considerable sum of money for which he was unable to account beyond trying to claim he'd made it selling things. Otero had just that much money on him at the time of the assault; later, he found this to be missing.'

'Are you sure of that?'

'Are you asking me to disbelieve the evidence of my ears?'

'I'm sorry, I've obviously expressed myself very badly. What I'm trying to say is, do you believe him?'

'Why should I disbelieve him?'

'Well, for one thing when I questioned him at his home, he made no mention of the missing money.'

'Naturally, I have made inquiries to confirm or contradict Flores's story. No one admits to having bought anything from either him or his woman. Further, one villager saw Flores near the Englishman's home on Sunday evening and another overheard the two talking about how much money they'd managed to steal.'

'I then conducted a search of the cave in which the couple have been living and I found a crowbar. This is the weapon he used.'

'I imagine you've had it checked for traces?'

'Do you take me for a yokel? There was none.'

'Which would suggest . . .'

'That it was wiped clean.'

'Unless it wasn't the weapon.'

'What would you seek before you made the arrest? A signed confession?'

'It's just that . . . Well, I don't think that's how it can be because the two assaults are connected.'

'My understanding until now has been that Señor Gore's evidence is that he suffered his injuries in an accident. Has he changed that?'

'No. But you see . . .'

'Superior Chief Salas referred to you as someone who preferred the complicated to the simple, chaos to order.'

'I'm sure one has to remember that in a village like Altobarí there is even more feeling than usual against gipsies.'

'Ignorance breeds prejudice.'

'But they can't possibly be guilty of everything for which they're blamed . . . Do you know countrymen? People from villages like Altibarí?'

'No,' replied Fiol, in tones of gratitude.

'They kind of see life differently. For instance, when they believe something, they'll never change their minds about it whatever happens and to support that belief they'll say things which aren't true but which, to them, are not lies.'

'Presumably, you've gained your knowledge from personal experience?'

'There is a logic to the way their minds work, but it's a different kind of logic,' said Alvarez, struggling to break through the ignorance of a city mentality. 'Prejudice, so strong and ingrained that to them it is proof, names a man guilty. But because there's a fear that he may escape the just punishment, men give evidence to ensure he doesn't. One claims he saw Flores near the señor's house, another that he overheard Flores and his woman discussing the money they'd stolen. We would say they're lying. But for all the villagers, and not just for them, they're making certain that justice—their justice—is done and therefore they cannot be lying. Do you understand?'

'I understand one thing. I should be even more thankful than I have been that I was not born on this island. I am a busy man, so I will say goodbye.'

As Alvarez replaced the receiver, he was reminded of the old Mallorquin saying: A fool was far too foolish to understand a wise man, but a wise man was far too wise to understand a fool.

'Enrique,' said Dolores, a snap to her voice, 'is the meat tough? Or perhaps the allioli is not quite as it should be?'

'Everything's delicious,' he hastily replied.

'Then why, when I asked you if you wanted some more, did you hesitate?'

'I'm sorry. My mind was miles away.'

'Tucked up with a woman?' suggested Jaime.

'Must you always expose your crudity in front of your children?' she demanded. But as she served Alvarez another slice of loin of pork and pushed across the table the earthenware jug filled with allioli she wondered. Where women were concerned, he was weak. Time and time again, he'd become embroiled with a foreign hussy. Worse than weak, stupid. Had she not named several widows with property, yet always he found fault with them. This one had a tongue edged with steel, that one had the looks to freeze a man's ambitions. As if either speech or appearance mattered when there were many hectares of land . . .

'Why does Uncle eat so much?' Juan asked. Isabel giggled.

'Be quiet,' she snapped.

'But he takes so long to finish. I want to go to Alfredo's to play.'

'If you're not careful, it'll be a long time before you go out again to play. Sit up; fold your hands and put them on the table; keep your feet still.'

No one disobeyed Dolores when she spoke in that tone of voice.

After a moment, Jaime, ever hopeful, said: 'All right, then, suppose you tell us what has got you daydreaming?'

Alvarez refilled his tumbler with wine. 'Before lunch, I had to have a word with Inspector Fiol. He's very clever so he thinks I'm stupid.' He smothered a slice of meat in allioli, ate.

'Then it's he who's stupid,' snapped Dolores, who permitted only herself to consider Alvarez a fool.

'He certainly doesn't seem able to begin to understand the way a villager thinks. You see, in this case a Peeping Tom was watching an English señor . . .'

'What's a Peeping Tom?' interrupted Juan.

'What did he see?' asked Jaime.

'There's no need to feed a filthy mind by going into details,' said Dolores firmly.

'He was knocked unconscious in the English señor's garden,' continued Alvarez. 'I know it had to be one of two men who assaulted him, but Fiol thinks I'm wrong and says it's a man who's been hanging around the village, making himself a nuisance along with his woman. Fiol's even more certain because one villager has told him he saw the man near the señor's house that night and another says he heard the couple talking about what they'd stolen.'

'What's a Peeping Tom?' Juan asked for the second time.

Jaime, indirectly expressing his pique at Dolores's attitude, decided to ignore her directions and answer. 'A man what hides so that he can stare at ladies doing naughty things.'

'Like when you look at the magazines Uncle Tolo keeps for you?'

Jaime, silently cursing his son, glanced quickly at Dolores. Her expression made it clear that she had heard, understood, and when they were in the privacy of their bedroom would comment.

Alvarez continued as if there'd been no interruptions. 'He simply cannot understand how the villagers' minds work. They're so certain the gipsy assaulted Otero that they're going to say anything that'll help get them arrested.'

'It was a gipsy?' asked Dolores.

'That's right.'

'Then it's you who's being stupid. Of course it was him.'

CHAPTER 10

The square of lint on Otero's head was smaller and the hair about it had already grown sufficiently to form a dark shadow. His mother watched intently, her expression as worried as the first time Alvarez had questioned him.

'You had thirty-three thousand pesetas pinched?'

'That's right.'

'Why didn't you mention that when I had a word with you the other day?'

'I forgot about it,' Otero answered sullenly.

'I suppose you've been off work since then?'

"Course I have. The doctor says it'll be at least another couple of weeks before I can go back. I'm still getting terrible headaches.'

'He could've been killed,' his mother said as she reached over to put her hand on his. She showed no distress when he roughly pushed her hand away.

'What kind of work do you do?'

'I'm a carpenter.'

'Félix, who owns the carpenter's shop, says he's very good at his work.' Her tone was proud.

'I'm sure he is,' said Alvarez. 'And it's as safe a job as any since there'll always be work that needs doing.' He turned back to Otero. 'So you've a good job and are living at home. That means you can save quite a bit?'

'He should, but he doesn't,' said his mother, and it became clear that this was a subject which vexed her. 'When he wants to marry . . .'

'Forget it,' muttered Otero nervously.

'I will not! One day, you'll meet a girl with the sense to

know a good man when she sees one and who isn't just interested in going to bars and dressing like a puta.' She said to Alvarez: 'I tell him over and over again, a man needs money when he marries. Children come from heaven, but heaven doesn't pay the bills. He won't listen and spends everything . . .' Her words were critical, her tone was not; a young woman must lead a chaste and sober life, but a man . . .

Had she managed to persuade herself that her son's Peeping Tom activities were no more than a harmless, eccentric pleasure? 'Then I guess he's the same as the rest of us, empty pockets when it's near payday?'

'Just like his father, God rest his soul.' Her tone became confidential. 'Sometimes, like last month, he even has to come to me for a little loan.'

'Yet on Sunday night, the first of the month, when he couldn't have been paid, he claims he was robbed of thirty-three thousand pesetas?'

Otero cursed. She was bewildered because Alvarez had been so nice and friendly and she'd forgotten he was a detective . . .

'Let's sort out a few things together,' said Alvarez. 'Because gipsies are blamed for any trouble that occurs when they're around, everyone in the village is certain it was Flores who attacked you because he reckoned you must have some money on you. In the face of such overwhelming certainty, no one can really blame you for going along with them. But since you didn't see who laid you out, you couldn't give any evidence that would help prove him guilty until you learned that thirty-three thousand had been found in his possession. That gave you the chance to make certain he was arrested. You claimed you'd had that sum on you and that it had disappeared when you'd regained consciousness. But there's something you must understand now. I know it was not Flores who attacked

you. So you've got to stop giving false evidence against
him.'

'I've told the truth,' Otero shouted.

Alvarez ordered a Soberano and then closely watched the
barman to make certain he poured a proper sized drink
from the right bottle; given half a chance, he would—since
Alvarez, in Altobarí, was a forastero—serve a short
measure of an inferior brandy. Satisfied, Alvarez carried
the glass over to one of the tables and sat. He lit a cigarette.
Each of the three men he'd questioned had stuck to his
story, no matter how hard he'd pleaded for the other to
admit the truth for the sake of an innocent man. Otero's
motives had been more complicated than those of the other
two. Not only had he been influenced by popular emotions,
he was known to be a Peeping Tom. Normally, he would not
be publicly branded as such unless he preyed on someone in
the village. But should he have to admit his infamy in court,
it would be broadcast to the world and bring mockery to
the village, whereupon he would become a social outcast.
So he had to provide some cause for the assault which
would hide his peeping . . . The other two, who claimed to
have seen Flores close to Ca'n Renato and to have heard
him and his woman discuss the money they'd stolen, had
simply wanted to make certain he was punished for the
crime they knew he must have committed . . .

Flores had been found in possession of thirty-three thousand
pesetas. That money had certainly not come from selling things
in the village. Although—despite their brave words—many of
the women would have bought something from the gipsy
couple in order to avoid the evil eye—a gipsy's curse could
make a woman barren or cause her face to become unsightly
from warts—their purchases in total could not have begun to
amount to that sum. So the logical conclusion had to be that
the money had been stolen. But not from Otero.

Alvarez drained the glass, had it refilled. He lit another cigarette. He wished he could stop asking himself so many questions since they provoked only mental confusion. It had to be wrong that a man should be found guilty on false evidence because he was the victim of prejudice. Yet was the degree of wrong lessened if he had committed a crime, but not the one for which he was charged? But surely there could be no comparison between a simple theft and a theft aggravated by a vicious assault?

He finished his drink, left the bar. The heat, trapped first by the valley and then by the houses, made him sweat before he'd taken half a dozen steps down the very narrow road which brought him to the small square in front of the church. On the far side were seven stalls; six were tended by middle-aged or elderly women who, when not serving customers with fruit or vegetables, gossiped vociferously, the seventh, which was semi-permanent, by a girl in her teens, dressed in the latest fashion, who appeared to be more interested in listening to pop music on the radio than in selling ice-cream or that most delicious of hot weather drinks, granizado.

He spoke to the woman behind the first stall. Could she tell him where was the cave in which the gipsies were living? She shook her head, her manner antagonistic because he was a policeman whose questions threatened to expose the village's shame.

He returned to his car and after following one set of directions which proved to be wrong—deliberately so, he was convinced—he found the municipal police station. The younger of the two policemen present reluctantly admitted that the cave was at the southern end, on the right-hand side, of the valley.

Alvarez drove out of the village, condemning the inhabitants for their prejudiced minds yet knowing in his heart that one would not have to go back many years to find the same attitudes in Llueso. Four caves became visible as he rounded an outcrop of rock and a further half-kilometre brought him abreast of them. He parked in the entrance to a field, climbed over a broken-down gate, and walked across a rock-strewn field in which a few hungry sheep searched, without much hope, for something to eat. He began to climb. It was not a steep slope, yet inside a few metres he was panting heavily and sweat rolled down his face and chest. Sweet Mary, he promised himself, he really would smoke and drink much less, take plenty of regular exercise, and regain at least a little of his youth . . .

In the last cave, considerably larger than the first three, there was a bundle of old clothes and some rubbish. As his eyes became accustomed to the gloom, he identified the old clothes as a woman whose face had been seamed by a harsh life and the rubbish as a single ring burner, a gas canister, a kettle, some tins, cutlery and crockery, and a plastic milk bottle container. She had drawn herself up into a tight defensive ball, her hands around her trousered legs. She stared up at him, her oval, simian face expressing both fear and a sly cunning. 'May I come in?' he asked.

Astonished by the polite request when she had expected nothing but rude belligerence, she said nothing and did not move.

He entered. There was a faint but pervasive smell which he could not identify. Perhaps it was fear and despair. 'My name's Enrique Alvarez, of the Cuerpo General de Policia.'

She looked as if she wished she had the courage to spit. 'I'm here to try and help.'

She spoke wildly in a language he did not know. But if he could not understand her words, he could their general meaning. Authority could only hurt, not help.

He took a pack of cigarettes from his pocket. 'Do you smoke?'

She gave no answer.

He proffered the pack, certain she was hungry for a cigarette. She reached out and grabbed one. He lit a match,
settled on some dried grass which had been laid on the floor
of the cave. 'What's your name?'

'Julia.'

She had spoken too readily and he was certain this was not
her true name. He remembered being told a gipsy never gave
his or her real name except to a friend because to know it was
to have the person in one's power. 'I've come to ask some
questions, the answers to which may help your man.'

'He didn't do it.'

When she spoke Castilian, her accent was so thick that
he had to concentrate to understand her. 'Do you remember
the night Vicente Otero was assaulted?'

'José didn't do that.'

'I know he didn't. But the problem is this: what I believe
or know is not important because it is not my case. So what
I'm trying to do is to find the evidence that will convince
Inspector Fiol that José's innocent. Tell me, where was he
that night?'

'Here.'

'From when?'

'From dark until light.'

'Did anyone visit you who could verify that?'

Her scorn for the question was immediate. Did he think
they led a social life?

'Do you know that one of the villagers says he saw José
near the house of the English señor that night?'

'The pig lies.'

'And another says he overheard you and José talking
about the money he'd stolen from Otero?'

She faced him briefly, her features screwed up from the
effort of trying to make him understand the stupidity of the
evidence. 'Do you think we would talk about such things
in front of them?'

'Otero says he had thirty-three thousand pesetas on him before the assault and after he recovered consciousness that was all gone. When Inspector Fiol searched José, he was in possession of thirty-three thousand pesetas.'

Her cigarette was now too short to be held in her fingers; she reached out and picked up a pin on which she speared the stub.

'Where did that money come from?'

She drew on the cigarette.

'If José is to be cleared of stealing the money from Otero, and of assaulting him, I have to know where that thirty-three thousand came from.'

'We sold things in the village.'

'But didn't make anything like that amount.'

She drew on the cigarette one last time, cleared away a little of the dried grass and stubbed out the cigarette in the dust on the floor.

'He'd stolen that money, hadn't he, but not from Otero?'

She screamed curses at him.

She looked so evil that he silently called on the forces of light to protect him. 'Can't you understand that I'm not trying to make you betray him? All the time it appears he was in possession of the exact amount that Otero claims was stolen, he must be found guilty. It's only if he admits where it really did come from, proving Otero to be a liar, that he can show he's innocent of the assault.'

She suddenly came to her feet, raced out. By the time he'd reached the mouth of the cave, she was a couple of hundred metres away. He made his way back to the Ibiza. Would Flores be any more ready to understand?

When built, the prison had been outside Palma, but the city had expanded to enclose it. Now, the inmates could look out and with bitter envy watch the world, and the world with righteous satisfaction could look in. Designed to hold persons on remand, it was not large; due to the never-ending delays of the law, it was never less than over-crowded.

Alvarez parked in the rough square beyond the main gates, crossed to the door to the right of the gates and rang the bell. He showed his warrant card and said he wanted to speak to the assistant governor. He apologized to the other for not having made the formal request to interview a prisoner on remand which the rules demanded, said that fresh evidence was to hand which needed checking immediately as the case involved a foreigner who was threatening to cause trouble through his consulate. Yes, the superior chief had authorized this unorthodox approach . . .

He waited in one of the interview rooms and after a while Flores was brought in by a warder. 'You're welcome to him,' said the warder with crass humour before he left.

'Sit down,' said Alvarez pleasantly, pointing to the chair on the far side of the scarred table. If looks were any indication of a man's character, he thought, Flores was guilty of every crime in the book and even some that weren't. Short, thin, swarthy, he had a scar on the right cheek which puckered up that side and added an expression of sly, vicious cunning. 'Do you smoke?' He brought out of his pocket a pack of cigarettes, put this on the table. 'Keep them if you're short.'

Flores pocketed the pack without a word of thanks.

'I was instructed initially to investigate the case because Señor Gore is an Englishman. My inquiries make me certain you didn't assault Vicente Otero or steal anything from him.'

'Then why the bleeding hell am I here?' demanded Flores, speaking with a similar thick accent to his companion.

'Inspector Fiol is now in charge of your case and until he's convinced of your innocence, you won't be released.

Give me the evidence I need and I'll be able to persuade
him you're not guilty of assaulting Otero. Where were you
that Sunday night?'

'At home.'

'You mean the cave? Were you there all night?'

'From dark until light,' he replied, unknowingly echoing
the woman's words.

'Do you know where Señor Gore lives?'

'No.'

'Do you know Vicente Otero?'

'No.'

'Inspector Fiol found you in possession of thirty-three
thousand pesetas. Where did that money come from?'

'We sold things.'

'I've spoken to villagers,' said Alvarez, deciding to bluff,
'to find out how much they paid you; the total isn't more
than five thousand. You've been buying food—there are all
those tins in the cave . . .'

'You've been there?'

Alvarez was surprised by the vehemence with which the
question was put. 'Yes.'

Flores, in the same harsh language the woman had used,
spoke wildly; spittle slid down from the corners of his lips
until he wiped it away with the sleeve of the dirty, patched
shirt he was wearing.

Alvarez could see no reason for the sudden fury. 'You'll
have spent all you made, so where did the thirty-three thousand cash come from?'

'We sold things.'

'You stole it. But not from Otero.'

Suddenly, and with such unctuous servility that the effect
was to repulse, Flores said: 'Señor, I could never lie to a
great man like you. I swear on the grave of my mother that
I am telling the truth. That money came from what we
sold.'

Hiding his distaste for the other's manner, Alvarez said: 'If you stick to your present story, you're bound to be nailed a liar. No one will believe you can legitimately have made that sort of money. But tell me the truth and I'll prove it's Otero who's lying when he claims he had thirty-three thousand on him before he was knocked unconscious. And since there's no other direct evidence against you—the villager who claims to have seen you near the señor's house and the other who says he overheard you talking about how much you'd stolen will retract their evidence as soon as it becomes obvious Otero has been branded a liar—you will have to be released on this charge.'

'If I . . .' Flores abruptly stopped.

'If you stole that money from someone else, you're going to have to name that person. Which means, of course, you'll be charged with the theft. But surely it's obvious that to be tried only for theft is far preferable to being tried for a vicious assault as well as theft?'

'I never steal; never, never . . . Don Alvarez, I get down on my knees to beg you to . . .'

'Just stay sitting,' said Alvarez curtly, no longer able to conceal his dislike of the other.

'By my father's honour, I tell you the truth.'

He wondered if Flores had ever willingly told the truth about anything? What did seem certain was that Flores could not, or would not, understand that the circumstances demanded he now admitted to it. He sighed as he stood, bringing the interview to an end. The Menorquins had a saying, Honour is more important than common sense. But everyone knew that the Menorquins, like the gipsies, lacked both.

CHAPTER 11

Alvarez watched a fly walk across the desk, come to a stop, and then hunker down to sleep. His eyelids became heavy and he settled more comfortably in the chair . . . The telephone disturbed both him and the fly.

'What the devil's going on?' demanded Salas, as abruptly discourteous as ever.

'In what way, señor?'

'In every goddamn way. How is it you can never find the time, energy, and ability efficiently to investigate matters within your own department, yet have not the slightest hesitation or trouble in interfering at length in another department's affairs which are of no concern whatsoever of yours?'

'Are you referring to Vicente Otero?'

'Have you been interfering in so many cases that it's difficult to identify the one I'm talking about?'

'Señor, with respect, "interfering" isn't a just word when it was you who ordered me to question Señor Gore.'

'I am well aware of that. I am also very conscious of the fact that I failed to order you what not to do. As a consequence of which omission, and due to your natural affinity for chaos, you have managed to make a cat's cradle of the case. Inspector Fiol has informed me that due to your bumbling inquiries, most of the villagers are now refusing to give any evidence and the gipsy woman has disappeared. And just what the devil do you mean by taking my name in vain?'

The sudden apparent change of conversation momentarily confused Alvarez. 'I . . . I don't understand.'

'Then it wasn't you who went to Tabori prison yesterday

and quoted my authority in order to gain permission to speak to Flores?'

'As a matter of fact, señor, that was me.' Gloomily he realized that for once there had not been a total lack of communication between government departments. Truly, if a man were born under an unlucky star, he could never hope to dance with angels.

'Remind me of when I gave you such authority.'

'Señor, I had to speak with Flores to prove that he wasn't lying even though he wasn't telling the truth, and that Otero and the other villagers weren't telling the truth even though they weren't lying.'

'A task that most would find logically impossible.'

'Otero's assault was not the result of casual opportunity, but because there had to be no witness to what was about to happen to Señor Gore. This means Flores couldn't have been the assailant because he'd no motive for attacking the señor. Otero could not have had thirty-three thousand pesetas on him; he claims that he did, however, in order to inculpate Flores and his motive is no stronger than that Flores is a gipsy. Flores could only have had that money on him because he'd stolen it, but not from Otero ... Unfortunately, I could not persuade him to admit that fact.'

'Undoubtedly because, like me, he had no idea what it was you were saying. Do you now claim it was Macadie who assaulted Señor Gore, even though Señor Gore insists that he suffered his injuries in an accident?'

'Yes, señor. Sir Donald Macadie was determined to seek revenge. He went to Señor Gore's house on the Sunday night and found Otero outside, hoping to peep. Since he could not afford to have an eye-witness—for his own sake and to save his wife's reputation—he knocked Otero unconscious. Unfortunately, he had no idea that the force with which he struck might well prove fatal.'

'I wonder if it has occurred to you that all this is contrary not only to the evidence of every witness, but also to all the physical evidence?'

'I don't know that that's strictly true . . .'

'Further, if Sir Macadie did assault Señor Gore, he was doing no more than behave like a man; if Señor Gore wishes to try to make amends for his actions by claiming his injuries were received in an accident, I can see no reason for denying him.'

'That would be fine were it not for Flores.'

'Damnit, I thought you were claiming there could be no connection between Flores and Señor Gore?'

'Which is why the two cases have to be connected.'

There was a long silence.

'It's like this, señor. If I am right and Señor Gore is lying about the cause of his injuries . . .'

'Frankly, I am unwilling to suffer a repeated explanation . . . You will cease all inquiries into the cause of Señor Gore's injuries, you will cease all inquiries into the cause of Otero's injuries, you will cease all inquiries into the theft committed by the gipsy; in other words, you will not burden Inspector Fiol with any further assistance.' He cut the connection.

Alvarez leaned down and pulled open the bottom right-hand drawer of the desk. About to bring out the bottle of brandy and a glass, he checked the movement. Had he not promised himself to cut back on smoking and drinking? . . . But there were times when events beyond a man's control made it necessary to put even the most solemn promises on hold. He poured himself a very generous drink.

He awoke, stared up at the ceiling, and decided that modern civilization owed its existence to the siesta. Man rejected it to the peril of his inner equilibrium. One had only to see the white, strained faces of the tourists from northern countries who derided the siesta in the name of efficiency to understand that they had lost the ability to live a full life . . .

He left his bed, walked through to the bathroom to wash his face in cold water. After dressing, he went downstairs to the kitchen in which Dolores was using a wooden spoon to attack something in a large bowl. He looked around him.

'Well?' she demanded.

'I was wondering . . .' He stopped.

'If I'd prepared cold chocolate; if I'd been out, despite my painful, swollen legs to buy you coca; if I had made certain there's membrillo to have with the coca?'

'Of course, if you've been too busy . . .'

'What woman isn't too busy when she has two men in the house who know only how to eat and drink?'

Women had never learned to enjoy to the full the benefits of a siesta.

'Sit down and stop cluttering up my kitchen.'

He sat. She put on the table a plate with a large slice of coca on it, a smaller plate on which was membrillo, a knife, and a mug. She crossed to the refrigerator and brought out a jug of chilled chocolate, filled the mug. He humbly thanked her. She ignored him and returned to attacking whatever was in the bowl.

He spread membrillo over a piece of coca, ate. The mixture of tart and sweet was perfect. The cool richness of the chocolate was velvet in his throat. There were times in life when all the elements combined to grant a glimpse of heaven . . .

Heaven never lasted, at least on earth. As he ate the last piece of coca, he remembered the problem which had plagued him so hard earlier on that it had taken him a full five minutes to fall asleep. What did he do about the Altobarí case? The obvious answer, of course, was to obey orders. That would make everyone but Flores happy and who gave a damn how that misfit felt? Unfortunately, he did. Not because he was sorry for the other—how could one be sorry for so unprepossessing a character?—but because he was certain that prejudice was dictating the case, not fact.

'Enrique,' said Dolores, and her tone was suddenly sympathetic, not arrogant, 'something is wrong, isn't it?'

'In a way. I've been ordered to do something, but I'm sure the order's wrong because it'll cause an injustice, even though that particular injustice will reflect general justice.'

'I don't understand.'

'I don't think I do, either.'

'Who's given you this order?'

'The superior chief.'

'And you think he shouldn't have done?'

'Perhaps he wouldn't have, if he'd had more faith in me. But I'm not clever, like Inspector Fiol. If I disobey the superior chief and he gets to find out, I'll be in the . . .' He remembered her dislike for strong descriptions. 'In the mud.'

'Then make certain he doesn't find out.'

Perhaps because they didn't have the capacity to appreciate truly complicated matters, women sometimes came up with simple solutions to knotty problems. If he telephoned Son Termol to find out if the Macadies had returned from their sudden holiday in Rome and, if they had, went to have a chat, how could Superior Chief Salas ever learn about that?

He parked his car and climbed out on to the drive. He stared out at the bay, turned to look across the mountaintops at the north coast and the sea beyond, so intense a blue that travel posters did not lie. To be rich enough to live in such a place . . . Was, he reminded himself, to be married to a wife who betrayed one. Did there have to be a worm in every apple?

He crossed to the front door and rang the bell. Enriqueta

showed him into the sitting-room, beautifully cool thanks to air-conditioning, and said she'd go out on to the patio to tell Sir Donald he was there. He waited, wondering just how great a hidalgo the señor would prove to be . . .

'Good afternoon,' said Macadie, as he entered through the French windows. He shook hands with a firm grip.

Alvarez had visualized an arrogant man, indifferent to the feelings of others, seeing wealth as power. Reality, even on the briefest of acquaintances, was a man essentially friendly and free of condescension, who enjoyed his wealth but not at the expense of someone else. 'I'm sorry to bother you, señor . . . Don Macadie . . .'

Macadie smiled. 'Titles can be complicated. For the record, I'll answer to almost anything that isn't too openly insulting . . . Now, where would you like to be, here or on the patio?'

'I would prefer indoors. I do not really like the sun.'

'Because, having lived in it all your life, you're far too sensible! Then do sit down. And may I offer you a drink? I can provide most things.'

'I should very much like a coñac, señor, if I may.'

Macadie, who wore a T-shirt over swimming trunks, crossed to the side of the fireplace and pressed a bell. Within seconds, Enriqueta entered the room. He said, in English: 'Would you bring a brandy and a champagne, please?'

Enriqueta asked Alvarez in Spanish what he wanted with the brandy, left. Macadie sat on one of the chairs, richly covered in brocade. 'I hope you won't mind if I say that your English is excellent and I envy you your ability to speak another language. I've tried to learn Spanish, but had the forethought to make certain the staff understand sufficient English. I suppose the national inability to speak a foreign language is largely due to laziness, but in my case I claim in mitigation that by my age one has lost so many millions of brain cells that all too often I can't even call on the English word I want.'

Macadie's friendly, amusing, self-deprecatory manner held true to the reputation the English had once enjoyed. Word of an Englishman had indicated the greatest good faith. It was some years since the saying had fallen into disuse. 'We have the advantage of using two languages from when we are young. If one speaks two, I am sure a third comes more easily than does the second to someone who has only spoken one.'

Enriqueta returned with a silver salver on which were a cut-glass goblet and a flute. She presented the salver to them to help themselves, left. Macadie said: 'I imagine this is not primarily a social visit?'

'Regretfully, no, señor, it isn't.'

'I hope I've not broken any laws of the land? But frankly, it seems it can be very difficult not to. My solicitor tells me that the laws are changed with such bewildering frequency that even he does not always know what's what.'

'I need to ask you about Señor Franklin Gore.'

Macadie rolled the name around in his mind. 'I don't think I know him. Of course, we might have met casually, but the Christian name, Franklin, is relatively unusual and I'd have thought I'd remember it . . . Presumably, you've some reason for thinking I might have known him?'

Alvarez took a deep breath. 'I understand your wife is friendly with him.'

'Are you sure you're not mixing us up with someone else?'

'Quite certain.'

'Where does he live?'

'Just outside Altobarí.'

'Which is where?'

'It's a village in the mountains, to the north-west of Palma.'

'Then you are confusing us. The only people we know from that part of the island are keen bridge players. Too keen for my money, since a missed trick is virtually considered cause for capital punishment.'

'Your wife has visited the señor on several occasions.'

'That is nonsense,' said Macadie sharply.

'Is the señora at home?'

'She went into Palma this morning and has not yet returned. Why do you ask?'

'I have some questions I must put to her.'

'Concerning this man, Gore?'

'Yes, señor.'

'I've already said, she does not know him.'

'I am very sorry, but Señor Gore employs a daily woman who has identified her as a visitor to the house.'

'Then this woman is grossly mistaken.'

'Señor Gore was injured just over two weeks ago and I am trying to find out who assaulted him.'

'Are you now going so far as to suggest that my wife was involved in that?'

'Of course not. But, señor, in nearly every crime there is a motive, so if one can find out what that was, one has a better chance of identifying the culprit. I am trying to discover what was the motive for the assault on Señor Gore.'

'Would there not be far more point in questioning him about that?'

'He claims he was injured in an accident.'

'Then I'm damned if I understand why you're here, making the most absurd allegations.'

'The facts indicate that the señor was assaulted by another person, but he is trying to conceal that fact because of the embarrassment which would be caused if it became known, not only to himself and his assailant, but also to a third party.'

Macadie drained his glass, stood, crossed to the nearest

French window and stared out. 'Were this England, I would phone my solicitor and leave him to deal with the matter. But since this is Spain, I am uncertain what action to take.' He swung round. 'However, let me make it clear that the inference you are trying to draw is as monstrous as it is ridiculous and that as soon as possible I'll take every step to have it dealt with as such. In the meantime, perhaps you'd be kind enough to leave.'

As Alvarez stood, he heard the sounds of an approaching car. 'Is this the señora returning?'

'Possibly.'

'Then I should like to have a word with her.'

'I'm damned if—' He stopped. Then he said curtly: 'Perhaps it would be the quickest way of bringing this nonsense to an end.' He marched out of the room.

A Mallorquin, Alvarez thought, placed in the same situation would have worked himself into a rage and have uttered wild threats. He would have felt more comfortable if he had been faced by these rather than by the cold, controlled hostility because rages were short lived, hostility was not.

Vivien, followed by her husband, entered. Like Macadie, she failed to match the image Alvarez had built up in his mind. Despite Aguenda's complimentary description, he'd pictured her as a woman on the make, using her youth, looks, and body to befuddle an older man. Yet it was the word 'restraint' which first came to mind. Her make-up was minimal, her dress was simple, and her only jewellery apart from wedding and engagement rings was a brooch.

She sat, said calmly: 'My husband tells me you are suggesting I have been visiting someone called Franklin Gore?'

'Yes, señora.'

'I know no one of that name.'

'I have spoken to Aguenda and she's identified you as a visitor to the señor's house.'

Macadie said curtly: 'Damnit, how much longer does this nonsense have to go on? If my wife's never met the man, how can a maid have identified her?'

'From a photograph, señor.'

'Then the maid's either mistaken or, for some extraordinary reason, is lying.'

'Señora, have you ever visited the home of Señor Gore on a day when you were supposedly attending a class at Sanidad y Eficiencia?'

'No.' Her voice had suddenly become strained.

'I have spoken to the señora who owns the aerobics club. She says that you have only once attended a class there, but that you offered to pay her very generously if, after that, she would tell anyone inquiring after you that you had been attending a class, but had just left to go shopping.'

'She . . . she's lying.'

'The señor earlier told me that you went to Palma today. Was that ostensibly to attend an aerobics class? If so, what will the señora at Sanidad y Eficiencia tell me if I ask her if you actually turned up?'

'I . . . I remembered something I badly needed so I went shopping instead.' She swung round to face her husband. 'Donald, I went shopping. I didn't go anywhere near Ca'n Renato.'

Sadly, Alvarez said: 'I have not mentioned the name of Señor Gore's house.'

She covered her face with her hands. Macadie said: 'Inspector, would you be kind enough to leave us alone for a moment?'

Alvarez stood. The stiff upper lip ensured civilized politeness even at so emotional a time as this—yet at what eventual price? He began to walk towards the door.

'You don't understand,' she said wildly. 'Franklin is my half-brother.'

CHAPTER 12

Alvarez sat by the side of the pool in the shade of a sun umbrella and stared out across the mountains. Macadie was extremely self-possessed. Then while his anger when he finally gave vent to it might burn more violently than that of a man whose emotions were on a looser rein, he would never act until he could be absolutely certain there was cause. Had he suspected his wife of infidelity, he would have had to be convinced of her guilt before he attacked her lover. A man who honoured loyalty as strongly as he would only have been that convinced had she admitted her disloyalty to his face. Had he challenged her to make that admission, she must have answered, as she had just done, that Gore was her half-brother . . .

Fiol believed Flores had attacked Otero in furtherance of theft. But Otero had never had thirty-three thousand pesetas and therefore there could be no discernible motive for Flores's assault . . .

Coincidences happened, almost as often as they didn't. But could one believe in the coincidence that Gore had been assaulted and tortured inside the house at the same time as a would-be Peeping Tom had been assaulted outside by totally different assailants? There had to be a connection between the two events . . .

He heard footsteps and turned. Macadie walked up to where he sat. 'Inspector, we owe you an apology.'

'No, señor. It is I who owe you a very sincere apology. But how was I to know?'

'You weren't. So I suggest we agree to let that side of things drop. But I imagine that now there are other questions you wish to ask?'

'There are indeed. But if you would prefer me to leave and return another day . . . ?'

'I think this is a matter which, for everyone's sake, should be cleared up here and now. If you would care to return indoors, my wife and I will tell you all that we can.'

Back indoors, Vivien began: 'I'm terribly sorry . . .'

Macadie interrupted her. 'The Inspector and I are agreed that all apologies due have been made and accepted.'

'Then I won't say anything more than that it's a relief not having to keep the secret quite so secret. But . . .' She faced Alvarez. 'Please, please don't tell anyone else. Because if you do, it could be so terribly dangerous for Franklin.'

'Señora, unless I have to explain the circumstances to my superior, I can promise you that no one will ever learn the facts from me.'

'You're very kind, considering . . . You've had to do so much because you thought . . .' She stopped, looked at her husband.

'I think another drink would be good for us.' Macadie went over to the fireplace and pressed the bell. When Enriqueta entered, he asked her to bring the Inspector another brandy, his wife and himself champagne. He then carefully initiated a casual conversation. It was another ten minutes, and after the drinks had been served, that he said: 'Well, Inspector, we're always assured that it's better to face the unwelcome than to try to avoid it, so what exactly do you want to know?'

'I need to ask the señora about her brother.'

'Ask away,' she said.

'Señora, why did you conceal your relationship with Señor Franklin even from your husband?'

It was only after several seconds that she answered. 'It's not going to be easy to explain because there are so many of the facts I don't know, but I'll do the best I can.'

She and her half-brother—they had different fathers—had never been close; there was six years between them and in character they were totally different. He had always been an extrovert and often sadly incapable of understanding other people's feelings. After he'd joined the police, she'd seen very little of him; after he'd transferred to another county force and she'd married her first husband, nothing. When her husband had died, it had been several years since they'd met.

She'd moved because she believed that a clean break from the past was the only way of learning to live with it. Not long after settling in Reppingham, she'd learned that Sir Donald Macadie was looking for a part-time secretary to type out a manuscript . . .

'I was very nervous about working for someone so important.'

'Piffle!' said Macadie.

'You don't realize that even in this egalitarian age, there's something special about a fifty-fifth baronet who owns an estate which goes back to Egbert.'

'I'm the twelfth baronet and the oldest part of the estate only dates back to William the Conqueror.'

'Only!' she repeated ironically. She turned to Alvarez. 'You must excuse our banter, Inspector, but it's our way of unwinding . . . Anyway, to return to what I was telling you and cutting a long story short, Donald conformed to the best traditions of romantic slush and proposed to his secretary.

'By then, my mother, father, and stepfather, had died and since both my parents had been only children, my one surviving close relative was my half-brother. The wedding was to be a very private one, but Donald and I wanted our near relatives to be present, so I decided to contact my brother. Having no address and only a vague idea as to

which force he'd transferred, I got in touch with his first
one and asked them. I then sent the invitation to the chief
constable of the second force, asking him to pass it on to
my brother. One of his minions wrote back to say that this
would be done.

'We heard nothing and he did not turn up at our wedding. Since it seemed he must have received the invitation,
his silence and absence . . . Well, I'm afraid it annoyed
even more than it upset me. It showed him to be completely
mannerless and that was very embarrassing.'

Macadie said: 'I never conceived for one moment that
his behaviour reflected in the slightest degree on you.'

'Because you're too generous-minded.'

'Because we choose our friends whereas it's God who
chooses our relatives.'

'Anyway, being far from that generous-minded, I decided
I no longer had any close relatives. Then, when we'd come
out here and were staying at the villa we rented near Palma,
there was a phone call one morning. Donald was out, so I
answered. It was my brother who was on the island and
wanted to see me. I refused to meet him. He then said that
he fully understood my feelings, but what had happened
had not been his fault since he had not received the invitation until some time after the wedding. And for ages
after that he'd been unable to get in touch with me to
explain his silence, but finally he'd been free to go down
to Stowton Park. We'd left, but one of the staff who was
caretaking had given him our address and he'd come hot-
foot out. Please, please would I change my mind and meet
him so he could explain why he wasn't the mannerless
swine he must have appeared to be.

'I felt I had to agree if it really hadn't been his fault. I
told him to come here so that he could explain to the two
of us. He replied that he didn't dare, for my sake. We had
to meet somewhere where there was no chance of my being

recognized and so he named a café in El Arenal . . . D'you know, it was the first time I'd been in El Arenal. I sincerely hope it's my last. Sartre should have finished his epigram. Hell is other people in El Arenal.'

At first, she hadn't been certain it was he who sat at the far table by a window. By now, it was a long time since she had last seen him, but it wasn't just that he'd aged, his whole appearance had perceptibly changed. But then he'd seen her and smiled. A smile never changed.

He'd told her enough to make it obvious she should forgive him. His time in the county force to which he'd transferred had become one of growing frustration because it had been the chief constable's policy that everything had to be done exactly by the book and so if an unusual problem arose, an unusual solution was not even contemplated, let alone executed . . . When he'd been on the point of resigning, there'd been a call from a special regional squad for volunteers for unusual work. He'd jumped at the chance of a move that offered excitement. After training for undercover work, he'd been detailed to pose as a discontented, out-of-work, bloody-minded man who'd lost his job for standing up for his rights and who in consequence hated all authority. His mission, to infiltrate a group considered very dangerous.

It had taken him months to establish his credentials, but eventually he'd been accepted into the group. What he'd learned and passed on to his control had so alarmed the authorities that the decision had been made to bust the group immediately, even though such precipitate action was bound to pinpoint him. So he'd been called in from the cold and the bust had been made. This had not gone according to plan and two of the group had escaped.

It hadn't needed a soothsayer to predict that he would be in danger. But retaliation was so quick that the attempt on his life was made before any decision about his future had been reached. Two shots had been fired at him and the nearer had sliced through his coat. At least that had had the effect of producing a decision. He was to be retired from the police, with full pension and a golden handshake, and sent to North-West Rehabilitation Centre.

It was after he'd arrived there that he received the wedding invitation and there was nothing he could do about that until he left. They gave him a new appearance, a new identity, and an account with an Andorran bank. The world was his oyster. But before he set out to discover whether the oyster contained a pearl, he had had to explain to his sister why he had not been in touch . . .

'He must be a brave man,' said Alvarez. 'Did he mention what were the aims of the group he infiltrated and why action against it was taken so immediately?'

'No. Naturally I asked Franklin, but he said he wasn't allowed to tell me; and even if he were, he wouldn't because it would be too dangerous for me. I've told you everything I know.'

'Except for one thing, señora,' Alvarez said slowly. 'I've noticed that throughout all you've said, you've referred to your half-brother or, more shortly, your brother, or to Franklin, but have never used the name by which you've known him for most of your life. Is there a reason for that?'

'There is, yes. He made me promise never again to call him that; I mustn't even think of him by that name.'

'But in the present circumstances . . .'

'Inspector, I have forgotten what he was christened and what was his surname, which, since he was a half-brother, was different from my maiden name. And should you think of questioning my husband at some later time, I'm asking him now to respect the confidence.'

'Of course,' said Macadie immediately.

It would not, Alvarez thought, be an exaggeration to say that when a man of Macadie's character gave his promise, even the Inquisition could never hope to make him renege on it.

She turned to Macadie. 'I've never hated anything so much as having to deceive you; but I had to.'

'Of course you did.'

'It made me feel like a traitor and a tramp. When I asked the owner of the aerobics centre to cover for me, I knew exactly what she was thinking.'

'Prurient thoughts come from a prurient mind.'

Alvarez stood. 'Señora, I should like to thank you for all your help.'

'You won't repeat to anyone what I've just told you?'

'Rest assured.'

When he left the house, Macadie accompanied him. That this was not merely an act of courtesy became clear as he put his hand on the door of the Ibiza to open it. Macadie cleared his throat. 'I hope you don't think that even for a second . . .' He became silent.

'Of course not, señor.' Alvarez opened the door and climbed in. It must be a very difficult world for a man of great honour.

CHAPTER 13

Alvarez sat at a window table in the bar of the Club Llueso and ate an ensaimada and drank a coffee into which he'd emptied two-thirds of a glass of brandy. Yesterday, Vivien Macadie had told her husband she was going to a class at Sanidad y Eficiencia which must surely mean that Gore had been discharged from hospital and returned home? (He should have remembered to ask her whether this was so, but no man could think of everything.) So now he could question Gore at Ca'n Renato . . .

He went up to the bar and had the glass refilled.

Aguenda demanded to know when the police were going to cease harassing innocent people. He began to explain, but she overwhelmed him with her opinion of the police in general and of Inspector Fiol in particular . . .

Eventually, he was able to get a word in edgewise. 'Is the señor at home?'

'He's at home, right enough. And there's no one would think he's just out of hospital.'

'Why's that?'

'Because he's entertaining. Without a thought for the feelings of decent people.'

By the side of the pool, a young and shapely woman lay on her back on a li-lo, her only covering a minute triangle of material which, despite the supporting cords, looked as if the slightest movement on her part would render it totally ineffective.

Gore came to his feet. He spoke with light irony. 'Not exactly a surprise visit, Inspector! Not after I heard from my sister . . . Deirdre, this is Inspector Alvarez.'

She regarded Alvarez through reflective sunglasses. He did not need to see her eyes to appreciate her indifference—nearly middle-aged, almost dumpy, definitely impoverished Mallorquin inspectors were not her scene.

'We need to have a talk, so you'll have to amuse yourself for a while.'

'Are you going to be long?' she asked. She spoke in a little-girl voice that was sadly out of place in the company of shocking pink lipstick, fish-scale fingernails and toenails, and a costume that hardly honoured modesty in the breach, let alone the observance.

'It'll take a few minutes.'

'Then I'm going for a swim.'

She came to her feet and made her way to the steps down into the pool. There was no second triangle of material.

'I suggest we go inside,' said Gore. 'I'm afraid Deirdre is not the most discreet of people.'

That, thought Alvarez, was like saying it was hot in July.

They entered the sitting-room, delightfully cool thanks to the air-conditioning unit. 'Grab a seat,' said Gore, as he walked over to the inner door and shut that. 'I can never get Aguenda to understand a single word of English, but I have the feeling that that's only so that she can jeer at my Spanish . . . Before we get down to the nitty-gritty, would you care for a drink?'

'A coñac would be very welcome, señor.'

He crossed to the cocktail cabinet. 'Do you like it with soda or ginger ale?'

'Just ice, thank you.'

He opened an ice container and brought out several cubes which he divided between two glasses, poured out a brandy and a gin and tonic. He handed Alvarez one glass, sat. 'You bullied my sister into telling you her secret and now want to know the answers to several questions?'

'I hope I didn't bully her, señor?'

He smiled. 'All right. The truth is, she told me you were rather charming and so obviously embarrassed because you were embarrassing her and Donald . . . Before we go any further, I'm going to have to ask a favour. Please don't broadcast the fact that she and I are related.'

'As I assured the señora, I will tell no one unless it has to be my superior and in that case I will make him understand the position.'

'Fair enough. So what's the first question?'

'Were your injuries caused by an accident?'

'No. Yet but for that blasted doctor, they would have been!'

'What did happen that night, señor?'

'I was watching television when there was a knock on the door. I'm always being reminded that this is the Island of Calm, so it never occurred to me to check on who was calling that late at night—I probably assumed it was Eric, my next-door neighbour who likes to do some of his drinking out of sight of his wife; I can't remember. It wasn't Eric, of course, but a couple of men who looked as if all-in wrestling was just one of their many hobbies. They embraced me warmly and began to describe all the things they'd do to me before they cut my throat with a blunt knife. Shouting for help wasn't going to get me anywhere because no one would hear, so I took the only course left and set out to confuse them. I asked them why they were so keen on killing someone who'd never done either of them any harm. They said I was the police spy who'd betrayed their friends. I swore my name was, and always had been, Franklin Gore, I'd never been in the police force, and the only thing I'd ever worked at undercover was seduction. They kicked me around a bit while they argued about what to do, then decided to check the facts with the help of lighted cigarettes. They tied my hands and legs, ripped off my shirt, and started. I gave a convincing impression of a man who felt pain more readily than most and who was such a coward I fainted at the sight of a dentist's drill. I screamed my head off . . .

'I was lucky on several counts. They weren't the two from the group who'd known me—presumably because it was much safer for them to stay hidden—and so they had to work from description and my appearance had been subtly, but noticeably, altered; they weren't very bright; in fact I have a good tolerance to pain; and although I say it myself, I am quite a good actor. In the end, I was able to convince them they really did have the wrong man.'

'They didn't decide to bury their mistake?'

'They discussed the proposition but, with more than a little help from me, came to the conclusion that, since the whole thing was a cock-up, assault was one thing, murder another. Murdered, I could become big news and the cause of an investigation extensive enough to make their lives very uncomfortable.'

'Señor, no assault on a foreigner is treated as a mere statistic.'

'Would you spend much time trying to identify two Englishman, guilty of no more than an assault, who must have returned to the UK as soon as a plane could get them there?'

Honesty kept Alvarez silent.

'Precisely! So they left me, sore but alive.'

'It would have been much better had you told me this truth at the beginning.'

'Better in practical terms? What could I have provided beyond two descriptions? And as far as they were concerned, I discovered something I'd only ever heard about before. When one suffers shock, one's powers of accurate observation go out of the window. Once I'd managed to free myself and was lying on the floor, hurting like hell despite my barrier to pain, waiting for help to arrive, I tried

to visualize them and just couldn't. Me, a trained observer!
. . . But what really kept me silent, of course, was the fact
that if I repeated the truth, I would almost certainly blow
my cover.'

'Was it not already blown?'

'Partially. And did I ask myself how and why! But the
point was, having convinced the two thugs that I was not
their man, I reasoned I wouldn't be troubled again from
that quarter.'

Alvarez thought for a moment. 'This makes it clear that
Vicente Otero must have been attacked by the two who
assaulted you and your evidence must clear Flores, so if
you will give me a statement . . .'

'I'm sorry. I've told you the truth, but I will not make it
official.'

'You have to.'

'Try and force me and I'll deny everything and revert to
saying it was an accident.'

'Flores's innocence depends on you.'

'I'll try to explain. But the problem with that is, how
does one make a blind man understand colour? Unless
you've been through the wringer yourself . . . When one's
given a new identity, the past has to be eliminated and
that's one hell of a job. Inevitably, there comes a moment
when one is totally disorientated. The person you were
no longer exists, the person you are to become is not yet
established; fact and fiction become inextricably confused.
I can still remember one morning just after I'd woken up
frantically trying to decide whether I'd lived in Sellinghurst,
which was the truth, or in Sunderland, which was the fiction. When I couldn't remember, I became scared that I
was going mad. We'd been given counselling tutors and I
went to mine for help. He said I was merely passing through
my FF and H period. Not flesh, fowl or good red herring.
I was in a mental no man's land. But very soon I'd pass

through that and the future would become the truth, the past the lie, and never the twain would clash.

'When you questioned me in the clinic, I was terrified that if I admitted my present life is a lie, the admission would catapult me back into the FF and H period. And this time, there'd be no one handy to help me through it.

'There was also a second, minor reason for not telling you the truth. I've made a lot of friends on the island. If they learned I'm not the man they think me, they'd start to wonder just what I'm getting up to and how dangerous it is to know me . . . You're probably now asking yourself, why am I doing what I claim I dare not do. First, after my sister had spoken to you, I was left with little option; second, reality has, as often happens, proved less dreadful than projected. As soon as I began to talk to you, I realized there was no fear of my mind going walkabout. And why not? Because you're sympathetic authority and subconsciously I can see you as a counselling tutor.

'So maybe you can now understand why I'm refusing to make an official statement? The next person I have to deal with might be all hostility.'

'Señor, your sister told me you joined a special unit of the police force and after training were detailed to infiltrate a group. What were the aims of the group?'

'I'm sorry, but that's classified information.'

'Then I have one last question. What was your name before you went to the Centre?'

'I have to disappoint you yet again, which is small reward for your courtesy.' He looked at his watch. 'Being a man who hates to cause frustration, I'd welcome the chance to prove there's nothing personal in my refusals. We're about to have a drink and lunch—just cold meat and salad—so would you join us to show there's no ill-feeling on your part?'

It was the first time that Alvarez had eaten in the com-

pany of a naked—or as near naked as made few odds—
woman. It made it difficult to concentrate on the cold ham
and mixed salad.

After clearing the table, Aguenda returned to the patio
and reminded Gore that her Mobylette had broken down
and he'd promised to drive her home. Alvarez immediately
offered to take her, adding that it was time he returned to
work. Deirdre clearly thought that an excellent idea.

As the Ibiza turned on to the metalled road, Aguenda
said fiercely: 'How can even a puta be so shameless?'

'Foreigners don't regard things in the same way.'

'Foreign men look at them in the same way as you spent
the whole meal doing.'

He hastily changed the conversation. 'So how are things
in the village?'

She replied at length that the other inspector was forever
making a nuisance of himself asking questions.

'That is his job, you know.'

'Even he should have the wits to know it was the gipsy,
so where's the need to ask questions?'

'Unfortunately, it's not as simple as all that. To start
with, there's the need for proof and at the moment what
proof there is suggests it wasn't Flores who attacked
Vicente.'

'Then the proof's nonsense.'

They were nearing the village and if he continued even
at their present very moderate speed, they would reach her
home before he'd guided the conversation in the direction
in which he wanted to take it. If that happened, the break
which arrival would cause might give her time to remember
that originally he had refused to accept the proposition that
since Flores was a gipsy, he had to be guilty. He braked to
a halt by a grove of olive trees so gnarled and hollowed out
that they looked as if they really might be the thousand

years old that tradition always claimed. 'D'you smoke?' he asked, as he offered a pack.

'Of course not!'

He lit a cigarette. 'Like I just said, it's difficult to find the proof that the gipsy stole the money from Vicente.'

'What's so difficult?'

'Vicente never saw who hit him and so he can't make an identification.'

'Doesn't need to, seeing the gipsy was seen near the señor's villa.'

'It's not the strongest of identifications and there's a problem with the times.'

'Then what about Agapito hearing him and his woman talking about what they'd pinched?'

'The courts often don't put as much weight on that sort of evidence as they should.'

'He'd the money, hadn't he?'

'But we can't prove that that money had ever been in Vicente's possession ... I know it must seem like we're marking time, but we're not. We have to produce sufficient evidence to persuade a court that Flores must have stolen the money from Vicente after knocking him unconscious and right now we can't do that. What we really need is to show that Flores's been on the pinch elsewhere. He must have been, but no one's come forward to tell Inspector Fiol they've lost something.'

'And you know why? Because he refuses to understand when they talk Mallorquin.'

'It's not a case of refusing; he just can't, because he doesn't speak it.'

She dismissed that as irrelevant.

'Are you saying that people have lost things?'

'Carolina had forty-seven thousand three hundred stolen.'

It seemed that she kept money in a tin in the kitchen

because banks couldn't be trusted. One day the gipsy woman had called, trying to sell clothes-pegs. Instead of sending the woman running, she'd felt sorry for the other and had bought some. She was only just sixty, but her mother had gone soft in the head at the same age.

'And the gipsy woman came back another day?'

'Turned up at the door and begged for a blanket to keep warm. Needed to keep warm in the middle of the summer! Carolina, being so stupid, went off to see if she could find an old one to give away. Even left the outside door open.'

'And the money went missing?'

'D'you think the gipsy woman was going to miss that kind of an opportunity?'

'When did this happen?'

She shrugged her shoulders.

'Was it before Vicente was robbed?'

She thought it probably had been. This was the confirmation he'd been certain must be around somewhere, but which until now had not come to light. The thirty-three thousand in Flores's possession had been stolen from Carolina, not Otero.

'If you've nothing to do, I have. So you can drop me off at my cousin's who's been ill and needs her house cleaned,' she said.

Alvarez realized that since he had trouble in explaining the facts to himself, he was certain to have far more in explaining them to the superior chief. So when the secretary with plums in her mouth asked him if the call was important—Señor Salas was extremely busy—his inclination was to reply no; but he discovered he hadn't the courage to act in so cowardly a manner.

'Yes?' demanded Salas.

'Señor, I need to have a word about the Flores case. I

am certain that the facts are more complicated than they
have seemed to be until now.'

'Seemed to be to whom?'

'To me.'

'Then we do not need to be concerned.'

'But fresh evidence has come to light.'

'Inspector Fiol has made no mention of that.'

'His problem is that he doesn't speak Mallorquin.'

'To people with sensitive hearing, that is not a problem
but an advantage.'

'But when he speaks Castilian to a villager, especially
since he has a kind of Madrileño accent . . .'

'Since Madrileños speak the purest Castilian, it is absurd
to talk about an accent. Why are you wasting my time
with this arrant nonsense?'

'I am trying to explain something, señor.'

'Then it would help if you kept to the point. Assuming
there is one.'

'Because of the fresh evidence, we are faced with a different problem.'

'What the devil is this fresh evidence that you keep talking about?'

'I was having a word with one of the villagers this
afternoon . . .'

'Have you been making further inquiries even though
specifically ordered not to do so?'

'Only very obliquely.'

'How does one make a very oblique inquiry?'

'It's only by chance that Aguenda mentioned Carolina
had had money stolen from her. I was chatting to her
because she needed a lift to her cousin's house as her Mobylette wasn't working—as they become older, they can
become very temperamental. The bike, not Aguenda, that
is. And, of course, I was only at Ca'n Renato finally to

establish how Señor Gore came to be injured. So you can see how it was.'

'No, Alvarez, I cannot see how it was. If, despite having a logical mind, it is possible to be totally confused, I am.'

'Well, after discovering certain facts, it had become obvious that the señora had to be lying and if she were, then so was he. So I put these facts to the señora and she finally admitted she had been lying and explained why. Her explanation made it certain that the señor's injuries had not been suffered as the result of an accident but, as Dr Molina has always maintained, he had been assaulted and tortured. The señor now admits that and says his assailants were two men from England. It must have been they who knocked Otero unconscious when they found him skulking around outside the house.'

'Have you told Inspector Fiol this?'

'No, I haven't.'

'Why not?'

'I'm afraid that he is inclined to dismiss as irrelevant anything I have to say.'

'He is an excellent detective.'

'Señor, the circumstances being what they are, Flores can no longer be charged with the assault on, and the theft from, Otero.'

There was a long pause. 'Submit the evidence to me and I will see Inspector Fiol receives it.'

'I'm afraid the matter is not quite that straightforward.'

'I wish to God that that surprised me!'

'Although we now know that the money found in Flores's possession was probably stolen from Carolina, a woman in the village, we cannot prove that Flores wasn't hoping to steal from Señor Gore and that that was why he knocked Otero unconscious.'

'Goddamn it, haven't you just spent an endless time telling me you can?'

'The trouble is that although Señor Gore admitted to me what really happened, he says he will not repeat such evidence in court.'

'Why not?'

'Back in England, Señor Gore was in the police force and some time ago he went into undercover work and was assigned the task of infiltrating a group—I have no details on them. Having infiltrated successfully, he learned something about their operations that was so urgent and dangerous, they had to be busted immediately. Since it was going to be obvious he had betrayed them, he was pulled out just before the bust. Two of the group unfortunately escaped arrest and subsequently an attempt was made on his life. That decided the authorities to send him to a centre where he was given a totally new identity. It is that identity which he uses on the island.

'Despite everything, security was breached and the possibility that Franklin Gore was the man who'd betrayed them came to the notice of the two active members of the group. They sent a couple of heavies out here to force him to admit the truth and then, without a doubt, to murder him. However, he was able to bluff and persuade them that they were making a mistake and he was not the man they were after. As a consequence, they let him live. That is part of the problem.'

'Why?'

'It raises the question, why isn't he dead?'

'The obvious solution does not recommend itself to you?'

'I'm afraid I can't be making myself clear. The two heavies used such force on Otero that only an unusually thick skull saved him; they beat and tortured Señor Gore with considerable skill; had he admitted his previous identity, they would, since they were professionals, have murdered him not only from revenge, but to eliminate the sole eye-witness. And yet, when he bamboozled them into believing they'd got the wrong man, they left him alive, able to name their motives and perhaps to identify them. That was very unprofessional. So why this contradiction? I'm sure that the answer has to be important.'

'In what way?'

'It has to do with the señor's refusal to testify to the true identity of his assailants . . . And if he continues to do that, we cannot provide the link in the proof that's necessary if Flores is to be cleared. When I asked Señor Gore why he'd refuse to testify, he gave me a very long and involved explanation and I'm not certain I understood it all, or accept those parts which I did. But as far as I can gather, he fears that if he publicly admits the truth, he'll have to face his past. And the last time his future, which is now his present, came face to face with his past, which was then neither the present nor the future, he became mentally very confused.'

'One can only sympathize.'

'But if he was that scared of the past, why did he voluntarily make contact with someone from it? And when I asked myself that question, I realized something. All his explanations were much more complicated than they needed to be. And using a screen of words is how many con men work. But why try to con me? So is his refusal to testify really due to something that we as yet know nothing about; something which will have to be uncovered before he can be persuaded to tell the truth which will free Flores?'

'From what you said earlier, the gipsy has definitely committed at least one theft in the village?'

'Yes, he has.'

'Then are you suggesting we prolong this inquiry solely in order to clear him of one theft in order that he be charged with another?'

'He is innocent of the more serious one. The need to

prove his innocence of that surely cannot be ignored on the grounds . . .'

'I do not require a lecture on the ethics of justice.'

'Of course not, señor. But as you will have realized, should we do nothing and the full facts ever become known, the honour of the corps will be impugned.'

There was a silence. Then Salas said: 'Carry out whatever inquiries you consider necessary to bring this blasted case to the speediest possible conclusion.'

'Then it will be in order to book before I receive your written authorization?'

'Book what?'

'My flight to England, where I am convinced the answers lie.'

Salas's only answer was to slam down the receiver.

CHAPTER 14

Alvarez stared round the room into which he'd been shown and could not remember ever having seen anywhere else which spoke so clearly of past munificence; even the tawdry furniture and furnishings could not lessen the grace of the room's proportions, the inspired skill of the carved marble fireplace, or the beauty of the view seen through the three tall, narrow windows. He crossed to the nearest window. One could tramp the length and breadth of Mallorca and not see in total even a tithe of the lush growth beyond. What was there to boast about on the island to begin to compare with oak trees which appeared large enough and strong enough to support the sky?

A door opened and a tall, thin man entered. 'I'm Julian Mowbray.' He shook hands. 'It seems you've brought some of your weather with you; long may it stay!' When his features were in repose, he appeared to be a discontented man; when he smiled, it was clear that he was far from mournful in character. 'According to the calendar, it's summer, but until yesterday the weather didn't know that . . . Mr Brand has asked me to apologize for his not being here to meet you, but he suddenly had to make a trip into town. He should be back at any moment, but in the meantime may I offer you some coffee?'

The coffee actually tasted like coffee and the biscuits were delicious. Were the English finally becoming gastronomically educated? Alvarez wondered, as he ate a second ginger snap.

'As I was saying, I'm afraid our first trip to Majorca was a disaster.' Mowbray smiled. 'I should have found out what kind of a place Magalluf was before booking, but the travel company's brochure conned me completely . . . But the second one was the exact opposite. Friends rented a large place for a fortnight and suggested we joined them. The villa was luxurious, the maid was a treasure, and the kids lived in the pool . . .'

A few minutes later, Sarah looked into the room. 'Mr Brand's back and he asked me to take Inspector Alvarez along.'

Brand's room was alive with the sunshine which streamed through the two windows. He came round the desk, right hand outstretched. 'I'm very sorry I wasn't here to meet you as arranged, but at the very last minute something cropped up which just had to be dealt with. I do hope Mr Mowbray looked after you?'

'Very well, thank you, señor.'

'Good, good. Sit down there.' Brand settled behind his desk. 'Now, before we go any further, am I correct when I judge from what you said over the phone that you would like to be given some information concerning a past student?'

'Yes, señor.'

'Then I must warn you that in normal circumstances I am unable to give any details whatsoever.'

'I naturally understand, but I am hoping that in this instance I can persuade you the circumstances are not normal.'

'Then tell me about things.'

'The case concerns an Englishman, Señor Franklin Gore.' If that name meant anything to Brand, his expression did not betray that fact. 'It began when the señor was found injured in his villa . . .' Alvarez succinctly detailed the facts of the case. He ended: 'And the one final question which perplexes me is why the señor was not murdered once he'd persuaded his torturers that he was not the man they thought him to be.'

Brand picked up a pencil and rolled it between thumb and forefinger. 'You are, of course, inferring that there must have been a breach of security here.'

'Not necessarily from here.'

'I'm afraid that if there was such a breach, here is the only source from which the connection between the two identities could have been established. Which means I can refute the possibility.' He saw Alvarez was about to speak, held up his hand. 'Perhaps it will be best if I just briefly detail what happens when a student first arrives. I meet him at the station and drive him back here and no other member of the staff is allowed to have the slightest contact with him until he and I have decided what his new name is to be. So the staff know him only by that new name. All papers concerning his past are held by me and no one else ever sees them; only in the event of my being incapacitated is my deputy authorized to have access to them.'

'Then it does seem difficult to understand how anyone could presume to have connected the two identities.'

'Can you be certain it could not have been coincidence?'

'I think I can be, yes.'

'Then where does that take us?'

'I'm sure that there is a mystery which I have not yet sighted—if you can understand what I am trying to say?'

'Of course.'

'And until I can identify what that is, I'll be unable to persuade Señor Gore to testify to the truth and thus prove Flores's innocence . . . Can you at least tell me what kind of a group it was that Señor Gore was ordered to infiltrate?'

'I never receive those sort of details.'

'But the police force he served with will have them?'

'I'd presume so.'

'Then will you give me the name of that force?'

Brand looked at Alvarez, his egg-shaped head tilted forward so that a large area of his balding crown was visible. Then he suddenly stood, walked round the desk and across to the nearer window and stared out, hands clasped behind his back. 'There are times, Inspector, when my job forces me to make a decision with which I do not sympathize—but duty has to take precedence over sympathy ... You are here, I judge, primarily because you wish to prove a man is innocent of the vicious assault with which he is charged. I have the greatest sympathy with such an objective. In the hopes that it does not make me sound condescending, I will add that I find it heartening to meet a policeman who is more interested in innocence than guilt. But clearly, if you are to gain the proof you need, you must first ascertain the previous identity of Gore and that demands a breach of security.' He turned, walked back to the chair behind the desk, sat. 'Because there has to be the possibility that the previous identity of a student could become central to a matter of life and death, there is a procedure which can be followed and under which I may be authorized to release the minimum information necessary. Initially, I have to be convinced beyond any doubt that it is vital to someone's safety that the information be provided. Then I have to submit the facts to a person in the Home Office of a rank of Head of Division, or above. If, and only if, that person agrees with my submission, am I authorized to give the information.'

He rested his elbows on the desk, joined the tips of his fingers together. 'I have, I hope, indicated how strongly I sympathize with your motives. But, as I have already said, I am not allowed the luxury of sympathy and must restrict myself to facts. The facts here are that there is no question of life and death, merely—and I say this with bitter irony —one of a man's innocence or guilt. I cannot, therefore, in any honesty submit a request to the Home Office.' He lowered his hands. 'I do hope you can understand?'

'Of course. It is very kind of you to have taken so much time and trouble to explain.' Alvarez stood.

'Do you have transport?'

'I got a taxi here. Perhaps if your secretary could kindly ring for one to take me back to the station?'

'My car is free until after lunch so I'll get someone to drive you there.'

Even on a fine summer's evening, Blexted did not lose any of its air of dull, dour respectability. There was not a building of light-hearted design, the streets were narrow and clogged with traffic for most of the day, and since the Middle Ages, the inhabitants had been noted for their xenophobia. Alvarez stood at the window of his hotel room and experienced a fierce longing for the harsh contrasts and sharp emotions of the island.

He turned, crossed to the nearer bed and sat, read the instructions for making telephone calls and rang Salas.

'Señor, I've spoken with Señor Brand, the chief executive at North-West Rehabilitation Centre. Although very sympathetic, he is not allowed to give me any information since the case cannot be considered one that concerns a matter of life and death.'

'You have failed to uncover anything fresh?'

'I'm afraid so.'

'But you have made every possible effort to do so? Then no one can ever point a finger at the Cuerpo.'

'But it also means that I cannot bring any pressure to bear on Señor Gore to admit the truth . . .'

Salas interrupted him. 'Return by the first possible plane and report to me on your arrival.' He rang off.

Alvarez replaced the receiver. It had always been a journey that could really only be justified by results. There had been none. Yet instinct—and how Salas would scorn that word!—said that those results were needed to unlock a problem not yet glimpsed . . .

If there could not have been a breach of security at the Centre, how could Gore's assailants have learned that he was the undercover policeman who had destroyed the group? Was that part of Gore's story a lie? Yet that was to accept the coincidence that there was cause for someone to torture him who had no connection with the group he'd infiltrated. Was it a lie that he had ever been a policeman? How to determine anything if Brand were allowed to reveal nothing?

He found it difficult to sleep because his mind remained so active. If only he could bring himself to accept that there could be overall justice even where there was specific injustice. Since Flores must have committed many more crimes than those for which he'd been found guilty, he owed justice; if now found guilty of a crime he had not committed, justice would owe him. Who could doubt that the debt he owed would be very much greater than the debt he was owed? But try as he might, Alvarez could not abandon the certainty that justice should be individual and specific . . .

And then there floated into his mind the memory of Gore, in the middle of his over-elaborate explanation of why he'd lied about his injuries, saying he could still remember frantically trying to make out whether he'd lived in Sellinghurst —which was the truth—or in Sunderland—which was the fiction. A con man's patter? Or the truth, inadvertently spoken because at the time it had seemed totally irrelevant?

CHAPTER 15

A taxi took Alvarez from Sellinghurst station to divisional HQ which lay on the opposite side of the market town. He entered the ten-storey concrete and glass building at ramp level. In the front room, a sergeant and a PC were manning the desk; the PC spoke to him, then called over the sergeant.

'Fred tells me you're an inspector in the Spanish police, sir?' said the sergeant, hoping he didn't sound as dubious as he felt in the face of such a claim from a man who looked rather like an out-of-work publican. 'And you want a word about someone who was in this force?'

'I can't be certain, but I think he may have been.'

'I reckon it'd be best if you had a chat with the duty inspector. But first, can you show me some sort of identification; just routine, you'll understand?'

He showed his warrant card.

The sergeant turned to the PC. 'Go and tell Inspector Morris, Fred.' The PC walked to the end of the counter, raised the flap, passed through and left by one of the inner doors. The sergeant said: 'It shouldn't be long, Inspector, but perhaps you'd like to take a seat while you're waiting?'

There were three low tables, on which were dog-eared magazines, at the far end of the front room. Alvarez had thumbed through one magazine and opened another when a tall, well-built man, with a face sharpened by a clipped, military-style moustache, came through an inner doorway, crossed to the counter and spoke briefly to the sergeant, then walked over to where Alvarez sat. 'I'm Inspector John Morris.' Alvarez stood and they shook hands. 'Come along to my room.'

They took a lift up to the sixth floor, went half way

down the corridor to a small room, made smaller by a large Victorian bookcase. Once they were both seated, Morris said: 'I'm afraid I'm not completely clear how we can help you?'

How did one gain the sympathetic understanding of a man who looked as if he were the epitome of English reserve? 'Señor, I do realize that this visit is not according to protocol as no request has been passed through my superiors.' Then he added in a burst of honesty: 'In fact, when I left Mallorca I had no idea it was going to be necessary so I fear that they don't even know about it.'

'No cause for worry.' Morris smiled. 'I'm not a great man for protocol.'

As the old Mallorquin saw had it: Never judge a potato only on its haulm. He became more cheerful. 'I am trying to identify an Englishman who until fairly recently was in the English police force.'

'That shouldn't be difficult.'

'Unfortunately, I don't know his name then and although he may have worked in or near this town, I cannot be certain.'

'That does tend to make things a little more difficult,' said Morris, with a touch of amused irony.

'The only information I have is that he was posted to undercover work and was successful in infiltrating a group which was considered dangerous. For some reason that group had to be exposed immediately and this made it obvious that he was responsible for identifying them. Unfortunately, two of the group escaped arrest and later they attempted to murder him. As a consequence of this, he was sent to Hawdon Hall where he was given a new identity. As Franklin Gore, he came out to Mallorca. Recently, he was tortured and it would seem clear that this was to make him reveal his true identity, but he claims that he was able

to persuade his torturers that he was not the man they were
after and so they let him live.'

'They didn't kill him to protect themselves?'

'No, señor, and I find that as inexplicable as you evi-
dently do . . . Señor Gore lives near a village called Altobarí. One of the villagers, Otero, is a Peeping Tom and
during the past months Señor Gore has unwittingly provided him with moments of interest. Otero was outside the
villa on the night the señor was tortured and he was
knocked unconscious. Because the señor initially insisted
that he'd suffered an accident, suspicion for the attack on
Otero fell on a gipsy, Flores. But I am certain that Flores
is innocent and I am trying to prove that and this is why
the previous identity of Señor Gore is important.'

'I think I've followed all that,' said Morris, somewhat
dubiously. 'But surely if Gore now admits he was attacked
and tortured by two men, that clears Flores? It would be
one hell of coincidence for there to have been two assaults
which weren't connected.'

'Señor Gore has admitted to me that he was tortured,
but says that if he is asked in court, he will deny this and
will revert to claiming all his injuries were the result of
an accident. In such circumstances, it would be difficult,
probably impossible, to prove Flores's innocence.'

Morris rubbed his sharp, pointed chin. 'That seems an
odd attitude.'

'Which helps to explain why I am so certain that there
is a truth which I have not yet glimpsed; and that such
truth has to do with the past of the man who now calls
himself Franklin Gore.'

'So what makes you think he may be from this part of
the country?'

'He once mentioned that there was a time when he'd
become so mentally confused he could not remember

whether it was true that he'd previously lived in Sellinghurst.'

'That sounds fairly definite.'

'Yet he is a man who—as we say—speaks with the
tongue of a politician.'

'A smooth liar? . . . I presume you've been to Hawdon
Hall to see if they can help?'

'I spoke to Mr Brand, the chief executive. He was sympathetic, but the rules do not allow him to give me any
details.'

'Very well, I'll see if I can help. No promises, of course.
Where can I get hold of you? Are you staying at a hotel?'

'I haven't made any arrangements as I didn't know how
long this would take.'

'If Gore was a member of this county force, very little
time; not many of us, thank God, become targets for assassinations. But if the mention of Sellinghurst was a blind
and he was in another force . . .' He shrugged his shoulders.

'Perhaps I should arrange to stay at a hotel?'

'If I were you, I'd play it safe and book in. Try the
Wilton. It's not as fancy as the other two hotels in town,
but there are fewer staff with little to do but hold out their
hands, palms uppermost.'

There came a time for most men when they had to face life
unflinchingly. In the large, but almost empty, bar, Alvarez
ordered a double brandy and paid with a five-pound note.
He stared mournfully at the change he was given before
sitting at one of the tables . . .

He was surprised to see Morris, accompanied by another
man, enter. They crossed to his table. 'This is Detective-
Superintendent Tatham,' Morris said.

'Len's the name,' said Tatham, as he shook hands. He
had a bluff manner; a round, flushed face and upspringing
eyebrows added to the picture of a man who substituted

blustering bonhomie for intelligence. It was a false picture.
'Sorry to butt in on you like this, but I'd be grateful for a
chat. What are you drinking?'

At Tatham's request, Morris went over to the bar to
order the drinks.

Tatham produced a pack of cheroots and offered it.

'I hope you don't mind, señor, but I prefer cigarettes?'

'One of the joys of smoking these.' He lit a cheroot. 'Here
come the drinks. If there's anything more welcome than a
tankard of real ale, it can only be the refill.'

Morris set the glasses down on the table, sat. Tatham
said: 'First, I'll identify my position. I'm second-in-
command of the regional anti-terrorist unit. For reason's
that'll become clear, as soon as I learned about the inquiries
Inspector Morris was making, I was interested. And
what he told me decided me to have a word with you . . .
Have I got the facts right? Basically, you're trying to
prove the innocence of a Spaniard who's accused of an
assault?'

'Yes, señor. Only . . . Well, it's become more than that.
In the course of the investigations, I have become convinced
there is also some mystery which it is important to solve.
Yet if you ask me for reasons, I cannot really give any.'

'Up to a point, I'll usually accept a hunch. So in order
to determine this mystery, you need to know the previous
identity of a man called Franklin Gore who claims to have
been a police officer transferred to undercover work?'

'That is exactly so.'

'Then have a look at this photo.' Tatham produced an
envelope and from it pulled out a photograph which he
passed across. 'I'm afraid it's not very clear, but it's the
best I could lay hands on. Is that him?'

Alvarez studied the photograph. After a while, he said:
'I don't think so, but it's difficult to be certain.'

'We had to extract head and shoulders from a group

photo, which never helps, and in any case, Hawdon pride themselves on being able to alter appearances to a consider- able degree. Still, I don't think it really matters. I've checked the records of all county forces and in the past two years there has been only one attempt on the life of a police officer who'd been engaged in undercover work and his name was Detective-Constable Townsend. He was a DC who was successful at this very important job, but who had black marks on his record which would probably have prevented further promotion; he found difficulty in accepting discipline all the time and there was a drink prob- lem. Two faults which, of course, became bonuses in the covert work—a bloody-minded boozer makes for a good camouflage.

'Let's accept that your Gore is our Townsend. Then the fact he was tortured to make him admit his previous iden- tity gets me very interested, but before we go into why that should be, will you first answer a question or two? How did Gore manage to persuade his torturers he wasn't Townsend?'

'He says it's because he's a fast talker and a good actor.'

'I'd have thought he needed to be the greatest since Irving. But let's allow that he is—why didn't they kill him to make certain he couldn't identify them or their motive?'

'I was hoping to answer that question here, in England.'

'But you haven't been able to?'

'No, señor. And nor can I yet understand why Señor Gore refuses to tell the truth to anyone but me.'

Tatham drank, drew on the cheroot, stared into space for several seconds. Then he drained his glass, pushed it across to Morris. 'Would you mind getting us all refills?'

Morris collected the glasses and carried them over to the bar. Tatham scratched the side of his thick neck. 'There are some things you're entitled to know because I need your help, but they take us into very sensitive areas . . . Will you fell insulted if I ask you for a categorical promise to hold everything I tell you in the strictest confidence?'

'Of course not, señor. And you have that promise.'

Morris returned to the table. Tatham picked up the glass tumbler and drank. 'How much did Gore tell you about his undercover work?'

'Virtually nothing,' Alvarez replied.

'Then that's where we'll start. We, in AT, began to hear rumours of a new group of anarchists, Liberation, whose aim was to cause so much trouble that society would become disorganized. I can't say that at first we were all that concerned. There are always whispers. Then there were a bombing and an assassination in very quick succession for which Liberation claimed responsibility and we homed in on them. The first thing we established was that they weren't anarchists, they were nihilists. Anarchists want order without authority, nihilists want disorder. The poor devils of victims wouldn't see any significance in the difference, but we did. It's much more difficult to target a group which has no clearly defined political or philosophical creed and to identify their likely victims.

'For a long while we made no progress in identifying the bombers and assassins and the media had a field day detailing our incompetence. Then we had a slice of luck—which ironically came through a mistake of one of our blokes—and learned a name which gave us a lead.

'In a matter of weeks we knew that Liberation was a very small group which, because its size and the motivation of its members gave it tremendous security, wasn't going to be bust by conventional means. So we decided to send in Townsend. It took him a long time to establish his credentials, but eventually they accepted him and he learned about their plans.

'Their reasoning behind these plans was simple and direct. When acts of terrorism carried out by other organizations occurred frequently, run-of-the-mill bombings or murders would not breed the belief that authority was powerless in the face of their threat. So they decided on an action sufficiently shocking to grab and hold the headlines. They worked out a plan to assassinate the Prince and Princess of Wales.'

'Santa María!' Alvarez exclaimed.

'The Prince had agreed to open a new university of languages, in the design of whose buildings he'd taken a keen interest, and she was to accompany him. Since the strictest possible precautions are always taken when a member of the Royal Family appears in public, it clearly was not going to be easy to kill the Royal couple—and as many dignitaries and onlookers as possible. But they'd realized something. In this day and age, no matter how much security, there's always one particular section of people who can be guaranteed to cause hassle and yet have to be accommodated— the media. Television crews who demand to be positioned anywhere but where they've been told to go, whose vans have to be here when all vehicles have to be there . . . Liberation decided to send in a team which would ostensibly represent a foreign TV company since such companies and their staff are more difficult to check. However, Liberation still spent very considerable time, money, and ingenuity, which included the full cooperation of an attaché on the staff of one of the South American embassies, on lining up a team with seemingly perfect credentials. They even included a Spaniard to talk the lingo if necessary and who knew enough about video work to look professional. Once on site, it was intended to park the van as close to the opening ceremony as possible. The floor and sides of it would be lined with Semtex and estimates suggested a fifty per cent casualty rate within three hundred yards because the van and equipment would be turned into shrapnel. When the ceremony was in full swing, the TV crews, osten-

sibly to find a better location for shooting, would move, but
leave the van, and then initiate the explosion by remote
control ... Faced with such a scenario, we had to act
immediately, despite the fact that this meant exposing
Townsend ... The rest, with one exception, you know.
And that exception is that recently there's been the whisper
that Liberation is back in business. Until now, we've had
nothing to go on to judge whether this is a false whisper, a
new group using the old name, or a revival headed by
the two from the original group who escaped arrest. Your
evidence makes me believe the last to be the most likely.'

'Yet if that were so, would not the two who tortured
Señor Gore have had orders to murder him once they had
forced him to confess his past identity?'

'That is logical. Which is why I'd been hoping you'd be
able to say why it didn't happen. As you can't, I have a
request to make.'

'That I arrange for you to question Señor Gore?'

'I must find out all he knows,' said Tatham with force.
'If there is a new or revived Liberation, we have to crack
it before they plan another assassination of Royalty. But to
do that, we must have information. Gore may have learned
something while he was being questioned; at the very least,
he can provide descriptions which could help us identify
his torturers.'

'He insisted he was too shocked to remember anything.'

'Then he's bloody well got to get unshocked!'

Alvarez spoke hesitantly. 'Señor, I will of course do
everything possible to help. But there may be a problem.
My superior chief is a Madrileño, which means that if you
ask for his permission to question the señor, he may refuse
on the grounds that Señor Gore can be questioned by a
Spanish detective who will be just as clever an interrogator
as any English detective.'

'So how do we get round that?'

'I could have a word with Señor Salas and try to make him understand that realistically only you can conduct an effective interrogation because only you know the whole background; I could also point out that your rank is far superior to the one Señor Gore held and therefore he is more likely to respond to you than to a Spanish detective. But frankly, the superior chief seldom accepts either my advice or my suggestions. So perhaps it would be best if you arrived on the island as a tourist and I arranged an unofficial meeting with Señor Gore?'

'I like your style,' said Tatham approvingly.

'D'you mind, sir, if I point out something?' asked Morris.

'That's what you're here for.'

'I go along with Inspector Alvarez. There's something going on which we don't yet know about and it has to be odds on that this something will answer the question, why wasn't Gore killed after he'd fooled his two assailants. Accept that and I'd say one has to go on to accept the probability that he'll refuse to cooperate unless and until you can home in on what this something is, which means you'll have to be quite positive he is Townsend.'

Tatham lit another cheroot. 'Only Hawdon Hall can provide positive proof.'

'Which surely they'll provide when it's made clear to them what's now at stake?'

CHAPTER 16

'You've told me enough to persuade me that this is a matter of life and death,' said Brand.

'Then what's the answer to our question?' Tatham asked, his tone sharp because of his impatience.

Brand looked across at Alvarez, who sat with Tatham in front of the desk. 'I don't know whether Mr Alvarez explained that before I can divulge any information, there is a set procedure which has to be followed? I make my recommendation to the Home Office and the final decision is taken by them.'

'Do you imagine they'll say no?'

'I find it difficult to believe they could.'

'Then . . . ?'

Brand picked up a pencil, fiddled with it. 'Would I be correct in thinking that you are suggesting I ignore the proper procedure?'

'Let's say, pre-empt it.'

'Is there a subtle difference I fail to catch? . . . A couple of years ago, Superintendent, I was unwittingly in a position in this building where I could hear but not be seen and I overheard myself described as the only all-living, all-breathing rule book.' He smiled briefly. 'While certain that this was not intended as a compliment, I have to confess I didn't find if as damning as the speaker probably intended. You see, although I hope I am not totally desiccated, I do see it to be cause for some pride that in this establishment the rules are observed down to the last dotted i and crossed t.' He put the pencil down. 'But I try never to let pride blind me to the seventeenth-century proverb which says that there is no general rule without some exception. Perhaps the seventeenth century had great need of exceptions since there were so many buccaneers around, on land as well as at sea . . . You have made it quite clear that your case now—as opposed to when I last spoke with Mr Alvarez—concerns the lives and deaths of the highest in the land; that it is essential for their safety for you to know whether Franklin Gore was Henry Townsend; and that time is important.'

'Critical,' said Tatham.

He stood. 'I have never known the Home Office to take time by the forelock, so I will go and find the relevant file.' His expression had hardly changed, yet neither of the detectives doubted it had been a very difficult decision for him to make.

He crossed to the inner doorway and the strong-room beyond, worked the two combination locks, entered, found the file, left, closed the strong-room door, scrambled the combinations, returned to his chair, sat, opened the file. 'Franklin Gore's previous name was Henry Townsend.'

'That answers that one!' said Tatham with satisfaction. 'What else can you tell us about him?'

'Presumably, you mean after his arrival here, since you will already know his previous history? Will you give me a moment?'

They waited, Tatham with obvious impatience, Alvarez with timeless patience, as Brand skimmed through the papers in the file. He looked up. 'An intelligent man, he had little difficulty with the course; his trouble stemmed from what I can only describe as character defects. He resented discipline—even though it was only imposed for his benefit—was moody, drank far too heavily, and failed to hide his contempt for his fellow inmates whose pasts had clearly been criminal. Since they inevitably formed by far the majority, he became something of a loner. Indeed, staff reports suggested that his only regular companion provided

a relationship which was most unlikely to be of benefit to
him.'

'Why's that?'

'This other man was . . . In his company, I could never
dismiss thoughts of Uriah Heep. Not in looks—I imagine
many would call him good-looking. But in his eagerness to
say the right thing, to praise, to please. I can remember the
morning they both left and sitting in this chair and thinking
how ironic it was that Gore was a brave, honest man,
Hickey was a con man who preyed on the weakest, yet of
the two I found Hickey the preferable character.'

'Which shows he's a good con man . . . While Gore was
here, did anything unusual happen to him or with which
he was concerned?'

'Not if one ignores the several times when he drank to
excess and caused disturbances. What kind of "unusual"
are you thinking of?'

'Frankly, I don't know. I'm looking for a needle when I
still haven't even identified the bloody haystack it's in . . .
Thanks for all your help, Mr Brand. And if you've the
slightest doubt, I can tell you, you've done the right thing
in giving us the information.'

'I rather think I shall only be able to accept that assurance if and when the Home Office eventually gives its permission,' replied Brand, with a bitter sense of humour. 'But
just before you go, can you clear up one worrying point? I
understand that in Majorca, Gore was attacked by two
men?'

Tatham turned to Alvarez. 'This is your pigeon.'

'They tortured him to make him admit he was Townsend,' Alvarez said.

'I know I have said to you more than once that it's
impossible for there to have been any breach of security
here . . .' Brand picked up a pencil and fidgeted with it.
'But surely this does . . .' He became silent.

Tatham said: 'It makes it virtually certain there has been a breach. I've been thinking about that. While none of your staff has any contact with an incomer until he has his new name, they see him before his appearance is altered, while it's being changed, and what he looks like at the end. Then while they can't connect names, they can appearances. So if a member of staff were shown a photograph of Townsend, he'd have been able to say what Townsend's name was on leaving, wouldn't he?'

'No member of my staff would do such a thing. I can trust every man and woman implicitly, Superintendent.'

'Which does your sense of loyalty great credit, but not your knowledge of the flip side of life. If I wanted to suborn one of your staff, I'd do it by one of two ways, bribery or fear. If your staff are as trustworthy as you believe, fear would be the more potent method. It's relatively simple. Choose the victim, kidnap a female member of his family, threaten to rape her repeatedly before murdering her . . . If your wife were under such a threat, would you sacrifice her in order to maintain your loyalty to your work?'

Brand did not answer.

'I intend no criticism, but because here you have to deal only with criminals who have some humanity left in them, you have been unable to realize that it is men who have none who prove that there is no such thing as absolute security.'

Familiarity did not breed contempt; it bred paralysing fear. As the engines revved for the take-off, Alvarez recalled photographs of planes which had crashed within seconds of becoming airborne. Desperately seeking relief from the horror of the moment—the drinks trolley would not be along for quite a time yet—he tried to force his mind on to something else; how was he to explain to Salas why he had stayed longer in England than expected without disclosing

the fact that Tatham would be coming to the island to
interrogate Gore? . . . And then, as the plane reached its
critical non-abort speed, he suddenly forgot what was going
on about him as he realized something which had been
staring him in the face since his last meeting with Brand
when he'd learned that Townsend's character—as summed
up by the staff at the Centre—had been about as different
as it was possible to get from Gore's character—as he had
found it. Dammit, hadn't he even once referred to Gore's
con man's patter?

CHAPTER 17

Alvarez signalled the stewardess and asked for another brandy. She gave him a calculating glance, as she tried to decide whether a third would make him belligerent, left.

He leaned back in his seat. He decided he now knew enough to plot the course of events; he might be wrong in details, but he would be correct in broad outline. At Hawdon Hall, Gore had been moody, bloody-minded, and a sot. He'd had to mix with his fellow inmates, but not to like them. Equally, they hadn't had to like him. Even a small-time crook turned informer had sufficient self-respect to resent contempt, so whenever possible they'd avoided him. Except Hickey, the con man with a highly developed nose for a good mark, a gift for manipulating another man's weaknesses, and the patience to absorb contempt if the rewards for doing so looked attractive. It had been very obvious that Gore had had access to more money than the average inmate and where there was more there was likely to be more again. So Hickey had targeted Gore's weakness by encouraging the drinking and showing obsequious admiration. Sober, Gore would have guarded his tongue and scorned the friendship; drunk, he'd begun to boast about the money that would be waiting for him and about his sister who had been smart enough to have persuaded some old fool as rich as Crœsus to marry her . . .

The stewardess brought him the brandy.

Hickey, by one of the lucky chances which so often seemed to favour those who worked the dark side of life, had left Hawdon Hall on the same day as Gore. What could seem more natural than to suggest a party to celebrate their 'freedom'? A party that would have continued until Gore had drunk himself into a stupor and could be robbed of all his identifying papers, specifically a passport which an expert could alter and a letter which was the key to a fortune . . . Con men were not normally men of violence, since their art called for subtlety, but if a rich enough prize came within reach and violence was needed to secure it . . . He'd murdered Gore and adopted Gore's identity, not very difficult because that identity had, in turn, been false. Even securing the money from the bank in Andorra had not been difficult with the all-important letter in his possession. So far, so good. But now he'd made his first mistake. Instead of being content with what he'd got, he'd been seduced by the vision of what more there might be on offer . . .

Moralists and humorists had always found the marriage of a wealthy old man to an attractive, much younger woman a source of material; a con man who could turn on charm at the first rustle of a banknote found the relationship equally interesting. Hickey had travelled to Little Sowerbury to suss out Stowton Place and the Macadies. What he'd learned had sent him hot-foot to Mallorca.

Softly, softly, catchee monkey. He'd settled down to wait for the right moment to make the Macadies' acquaintance, to be prompted initially by his assertion of friendship with her brother—who had wandered off into the wide world, who knew where? A man of strong appetites, he'd entertained freely, much to Ageunda's disapproval, while he waited. Then, after contact was made and he'd brought all his charm to bear, out went other women and in came Vivien Macadie. The affair had been carefully conducted since they didn't want the husband alerted. Also, to give him plenty of time in which to work out the perfect plan for getting rid of said old man . . .

Fate had stepped in to play the joker. Two men had turned up at Ca'n Renato, determined to wreak vengeance on Franklin Gore, who'd exposed and all but destroyed

Liberation. Initially, he'd sworn by all the saints, in none of whom he believed, that he hadn't been Detective-Constable Townsend. Then, when they'd begun to torture him, he'd been faced with having to make an impossible choice—did he continue just to deny he was Gore and suffer ever increased torture, or did he confess he had murdered Gore? The agonizing pain had finally forced him to cut the Gordian knot and he'd confessed the truth. In the event, they had let him live, for reasons he'd only fully understood later, when he could think far more clearly. If they murdered him, a full-scale investigation would he launched. If they let him live, they could be certain he would do everything in his power to prevent any investigation at all. And hadn't he done their job for them so that he deserved some thanks?

Had Dr Molina not been so pompously self-satisfied and determined to prove himself right (and perhaps, despite his protestations at the time, certain that Gore had gained his injuries from sado-masochistic practices), he, Alvarez, would have accepted Gore's version of events with a shrug of the shoulders and the brief thought that if man's capacity for wisdom was limited, his capacity for stupidity was endless . . . Had Gore's friendship with Vivien Macadie not been uncovered so that she had, in a desperate attempt to save herself, named him brother rather than lover . . .

As a nineteenth-century Mallorquin had written: Those who seek the future should research the past.

The depth of Dolores's relief at Alvarez's safe return was obvious when she told him that she had prepared Llom amb cames seques for lunch.

In the dining-room, Jaime poured out two brandies and pushed across a tumbler. 'It's good to have you back.' Then he lessened the compliment by adding: 'Since you've been gone, she's been worse than ever. The night before last, I was about to give myself a coñac when she started complaining about how much I drink. I told her straight, a little drink never did anyone any harm. So she grabbed the bottle and poured out enough to do no more than dirty the bottom of the glass.'

'You're not the only one to have been on short commons. D'you know what a tiny drink in England now costs?'

Jaime was uninterested in other people's problems.

Dolores, her face streaked with sweat, appeared in the doorway. 'Enrique, I forgot to tell you—' She stopped as her gaze settled on her husband. 'How many does that make?'

'It's my first.'

'And last.'

Conscious of Alvarez's expression, Jaime said blusteringly: 'I'll decide—'

'And what is it exactly that you will decide?' she demanded, handsome head held high.

He mumbled something.

She waited for a few seconds, then turned on her heels and disappeared from sight. Once she was safely out of earshot, Jaime muttered: 'She's becoming bloody impossible!'

Alvarez, critical of Jaime's craven attitude and unwilling to be drawn into the matrimonial in-fighting, remained silent.

'Why shouldn't a man have a drink when he feels like one? Sweet Mary, if he weren't meant to, there wouldn't be alcohol in the world.' He drained his glass, reached for the bottle, jerked his hand away as he heard movement from the kitchen.

'Enrique,' said Dolores, from the kitchen doorway, 'I have forgotten to tell you that the superior chief has twice rung to demand to know where you are.'

'Then I suppose I'd better tell him.'

'It's much too late to phone him now. I'm not serving a special meal for you to be so busy it gets cold.'

'Of course not. He can wait.' Wait until tomorrow, he thought. And although he must speak to Vivien Macadie, that also was not going to be a pleasant interview, so it might as well be put off. And until he'd sorted them out, there was small point in contacting Gore and telephoning Detective-Superintendent Tatham ... It was a sensible man who knew how to arrange his life.

CHAPTER 18

Alvarez entered his office, crossed to the window and pushed open the shutters until they were clipped back against the wall. He looked down at the street, half in brilliant sunshine, half in sharply contrasting shade, and watched the knife-grinder's van drive in the direction of the square. He waited and a moment later heard the Pipes of Pan as the knife grinder let the villagers know that he was ready to work. Years ago, he had been only one of the itinerant workers and salesmen, now he was the sole survivor. There had been the fishmonger, the olive oil seller, the toy and sweets man, the ice-cream man, the cottage cheese specialist, the buyer of empty champagne bottles . . . All banished in the name of hygiene or because their trade was no longer financially viable. It made a man feel old to have seen such changes . . .

He walked back to the desk, sat, leaned over and pulled open the bottom right-hand drawer and brought out the bottle of brandy and a glass. Two drinks later, he decided he was sufficiently recovered from his close encounter with old age to phone Salas. First, he told himself as he dialled, he'd give a general report and then, without betraying any of Tatham's confidences, an explanation of how he'd uncovered the truth . . .

The plum-voiced secretary told him to wait. Only seconds later, Salas demanded: 'What the devil have you been doing? Taking a holiday?'

'Señor, as you know, my purpose in travelling to England was to find the answers to certain questions, but this proved to be far more difficult than I had anticipated, which is why I have only just returned. You see, it turns out that Señor

Gore, who was really Detective-Constable Townsend, was not Señor Gore or Townsend, but was Señor Hickey before he became Señor Gore . . .'

'For God's sake, Alvarez, are you incapable of making a simple, logical report? Did you learn anything to suggest why Señor Gore was murdered last night?'

He spoke to Tatham over the phone. 'Señor, I promised to tell you when I'd spoken to Señor Gore and it would be all right for you to come to the island to question him. Unfortunately, he was murdered last night.'

'Was he, by God!'

'And if I'm right in what I have surmised, he was not Señor Gore, he was Señor Hickey.'

'As Alice said, things get curiouser and curiouser.'

For the second time, Alvarez explained the facts which had led him to his conclusion.

'All that raises one very big question, doesn't it? Why did the men return to murder him when they knew that he wasn't Gore, hadn't betrayed them in the past, and even more to the point, couldn't betray them in the future without exposing himself as a murderer?'

'I have asked the same question of myself several times and not reached an answer.'

'No intention of trying to tell you how to run your business, of course, but I think you'll have to find out before you can land the case . . . I'll send you all the information I can from this end and we'll redouble our efforts to track down the members of what seems to be the new Liberation.'

Through having spoken to Fiol over the telephone, Alvarez had built up the mental picture of a cocky little man, all-knowing, deferential to his superiors and condescending to his perceived inferiors. The picture proved to be remarkably true to life.

'I am awaiting reports from the Institute of Forensic Anatomy and the Laboratory of Forensic Sciences,' said Fiol. 'Which reports are needed to confirm the cause of death and to test trace samples,' he added, obviously deeming an explanation necessary.

Alvarez stared at the chalk mark on the floor, near the cocktail cabinet, which marked where the body had been. 'What was the time of death?'

'According to the police surgeon, between twenty-two hundred hours last night and zero two hundred this morning. With the usual proviso that the time cannot be treated as anything beyond an estimate.'

'Did you find any cartridge cases?'

'No.'

'Which suggests the weapon was a revolver, not an automatic.'

'Unless the murderer, knowing a case can provide damaging evidence, picked it or them up.'

'That's a strong possibility.'

'I am gratified by your agreement.'

Alvarez scratched his stubbled chin. 'Where was he hit?'

'In the forehead.'

'Fired from close to?'

'There was no sign of powder tattooing.'

'Perhaps that could have been washed off?'

'It is difficult to think of anything less likely.'

'Then it's all a bit odd.'

'Indeed?'

'The murderer was almost certainly a professional hit man and such persons, if given the chance, fire on contact or certainly very close to.'

'You astound me!'

'I think that that's generally the case . . .'

'I was referring to the fact that after a mere five minutes and a handful of questions, you know that this was a con-

tract killing! Is it an intuitive skill or one which comes
from extensive experience gained from your work on the
multitude of contract killings which take place in Llueso?'

Alvarez tried to introduce a much lighter touch. 'No
intuition, just lots of perspiration back in England where
I discovered that Señor Gore wasn't Señor Gore, but
was Señor Hickey and therefore not Detective-Constable
Townsend.' Alvarez explained the facts.

Fiol crossed the room to stand by the window. He put
his hands in the pockets of his well pressed linen trousers
and jangled some coins as he spoke. 'You are assuming it
was the same two men who previously assaulted and tortured the señor who returned to murder him? Why should
they, when previously they had deemed his murder unnecessary?'

'I've tried to find the answer to that, but so far can't.'

The jingling ceased. 'I think I prefer to continue with the
lines of inquiry I have already initiated.'

Alvarez hesitated, then said: 'Has Aguenda any idea
whether he was expecting someone yesterday?'

'Aguenda?'

'The daily, who kept the house clean and sometimes
cooked for him.'

'The Sitzer woman? I have questioned her, of course, but
that's a thankless task since she's mentally retarded.'

'I don't think that that's really the case.'

'We undoubtedly judge from different levels.'

'Perhaps it would be an idea if I had a word with her? I
might be able to learn something useful.'

Fiol turned and studied Alvarez for several seconds. 'I
have to confess that I do not understand the reason for your
being here.'

'I suppose the superior chief suggested it as I'd recently
been in contact with Señor Gore. Or should I call him
Señor Hickey? Anyway, the point is that what I learned in

England could add significance to something which otherwise would appear insignificant.'

'Because I'm incapable of appreciating its true value?'

'That's not at all what I'm trying to say. What I mean
is . . .'

'I am certain of one thing. You have now given me all
the assistance of which you are capable.'

In the face of such hostility, Alvarez said goodbye and
left.

He drove into the village and inquired for Aguenda's
house. It proved to be one of twenty, all abutting directly
on to the road and differing only in the colours of their
shutters and of the flowers in the window-boxes. He pushed
through the bead curtain to step into the entrance room,
spotlessly clean and smelling of furniture polish, and called
out.

Aguenda came through the doorway. 'What the hell is it
now?'

'I need to know one or two things. I take it you were at
Ca'n Renato yesterday morning, as usual?'

'And if I was?'

'Then you can tell me what sort of a mood the señor was
in.'

The question puzzled her.

'Did he seem at all worried about anything?'

She thought and then answered that the señor had been
much the same as usual. When she'd arrived, he'd told her
in his execrable Spanish that he was going into Palma and
would bring back some cold meat for his lunch, so if she'd
just prepare some cold boiled potatoes and a salad . . .
When he'd returned, he'd offered her a drink, which he
often did.

'And that's the last time you saw him alive—when you
left after finishing work?'

'Of course it is.'

'What happened this morning?'

Her manner changed and her expression recalled both the shock she had suffered and the frightened reverence with which a Mallorquin always met death. 'Mother of God, to think he'd laughed with me the day before, given me a drink, and there he was on the floor, dead!'

'It must have been a terrible shock,' he said sympathetically.

She fiddled with her dress.

'Tell me everything that happened, right from the moment you arrived.'

'The front door was unlocked, which meant he was at home, so I went straight through to the kitchen.'

'What state was that in?'

'Like usual, with all the dirty things waiting for me.'

'D'you reckon from what needed washing-up that he'd had guests to a meal?'

'There wasn't enough.'

'So you did the washing-up; what then?'

'I went through to the sitting-room to do the dusting and tidying.'

'Did you see his body right away?'

'Soon as I entered, since it was near the cocktail cabinet.'

'Did you check to see if he was still alive?'

'You think I couldn't tell just by looking?'

'What state was the room in? Did it look as if there'd been some sort of a fight?'

'It wasn't more untidy than usual, if that's what you mean? There was a newspaper spread all over the settee and the television magazine on the floor. And the bust glass.'

'What bust glass?'

'He'd dropped one on the floor, beyond the carpet, and it was in slivers.'

'Was anything else out of place?'

'Not except for the things on top of the cocktail cabinet.'

'What were they?'

'An opened bottle of whisky, a glass, and a soda siphon.'

'Was the glass clean?'

'There was whisky in it, but nothing more; no soda.'

'Did you leave everything as you found it?'

'Think I was having people say I didn't do my job right?'

'What did you do?'

'Cleaned up the broken glass and the mess on the tiles, of course. Put the whisky and siphon back in the cabinet.'

'And the other glass?'

'Took that through to the kitchen to clean it.'

'I don't suppose you've any idea who might have killed him?'

'Not with the gipsy locked up, no.'

'As far as you know, had he had a row with anyone recently?'

'He wasn't that kind of a man. If there was trouble, he didn't shout, he found a way round it.'

Ever the con man. But he hadn't been able to con someone out of murdering him.

Salas had ordered him to assist in the murder investigations, but Fiol had made it clear that such help was as unwelcome as it was unnecessary. So beyond having a word with the Macadies, there was very little more, if anything, that he could do. It was a thought that made for a cheerful drive home.

CHAPTER 19

Alvarez looked at the mountains, the sea, and Llueso Bay, and briefly pondered the paradox of a world which offered both this beauty and the sordidness of a murder which ended a murderer's life. Then he crossed to the front door of the central house and rang the bell.

'Isn't it terrible?' Enriqueta said, with some relish, as soon as she opened the door. 'The poor señora, losing her brother like that.'

'Very tragic.'

'Which reminds me, Mum said that if I saw you again I was to tell you Uncle Andrés died a couple of months ago.'

He tried to identify Uncle Andrés.

'It upset Mum.'

'Of course.' He finally managed to place the dead man as Enriqueta's mother's brother who had chosen the wrong side in the Civil War and had to flee to Argentina. After Franco's death, he'd returned for a three months' holiday and Alvarez and he had spent several evenings at one or more of the local bars. 'He died very young.'

'I don't know. He must've been nearly as old as you.'

Thoughtless people could be very unkind.

'When Mum heard, she said I was to go into black. But like I said to her, where's the point when the last time he was on the island, I was too young to remember?'

The attitude of the modern generation towards death—as towards so many things—had changed a great deal. In the past, a widow had worn black for the remainder of her life and relatives for a minimum of ninety days, after which they had changed into grey for another ninety; incredibly, a modern widow might wear colour within weeks.

'Will you tell your mother how sad I am to hear the news?'

'Sure.'

'Are the señor and señora at home?'

'Yeah, but she's been in bed all day.'

'Then perhaps you'd see if the señor could have a brief word with me?'

He followed her into the sitting-room and as he waited, calculated that, whatever Enriqueta said, Andrés must have been the older, by quite a margin . . .

Macadie entered the room. 'Good afternoon, Inspector.'

Alvarez noticed there were lines in the other's face which had not been there before; or, perhaps, had not been readily noticeable. 'Please accept my commiserations, señor. And understand that were it not necessary to trouble you at such a time, I would never do so.'

'Of course not. Thank you for your kindness. Please sit down.'

Once they were both seated, Alvarez said: 'What I have to determine, señor, is whether you or the señora know anything which might help us identify the murderer of Señor Gore.'

'If we did, we would have communicated it to you immediately.'

'If you realized the direct connection. But, señor, so often it is an indirect connection which is important and perhaps the persons immediately concerned don't realize that what they know can be even indirectly connected.'

'Naturally, I understand that. So if there's anything which I can tell you that might help, I will.'

'Did you speak to the señor in the last few days?'

'A couple of times, but only very briefly over the telephone and before handing the receiver to my wife.'

'Did you learn anything about his plans; where he was

going, whom he was seeing, whether anything unusual had
happened to him?'

'I'm afraid our conversation was almost invariably
restricted to conventional banalities.' He was silent for several seconds, then he said: 'I feel I should explain something. Despite the fact that Franklin was not only my wife's
half-brother, but also a very brave man, I was unable to like
him. My feelings were instinctive and without reasonable
foundation and I am ashamed of them, but, being a poor
dissembler, I was unable to conceal them from my wife and
thereby caused her considerable distress. She repeatedly
asked me to explain why I didn't like him and in reply I
could only fall back on Dr Fell.'

'I'm afraid I don't understand.'

'"I do not love you, Dr Fell, But why I cannot tell . . ."
An oft quoted translation from Latin. Naturally, my attitude has made events even more tragic for my wife, which
in turn makes me more ashamed of it.'

He was so clearly a man who did not normally express
his emotions that his explanation made it obvious he was
experiencing very considerable guilt at his wife's distress.
Yet, Alvarez thought, unknown to him, his feelings had
been both logical and explicable. Glad to have the chance
to remove the overwhelming but unnecessary sense of guilt,
he was about to explain the truth of the relationship when
he realized that Macadie was unlikely to gain comfort from
the knowledge that Gore had been his wife's lover, not her
half-brother . . . He felt his stomach knot at the thought of
how close he had come to so disastrous a gaffe. One day,
Macadie might learn the truth, but it would be from someone else's tongue. 'Señor, I should very much like to speak
with the señora.'

"Out of the question.'

'She may be able to help me since she will have spoken
to the señor at much greater length than you.'

'I'm sorry, but I have to be selfish. I view my wife's emotional state as being far more important than your investigations.'

'I understand . . . Perhaps in a day to two she may have recovered sufficiently for you to be able to ask her whether she learned anything from Señor Gore concerning what he did or whom he saw in the last few days? If so, will you let me know?' Alvarez stood. 'Thank you for your help, señor, given at so difficult a time. I wish I had not had to ask for it.'

'We have to do our duty, however painful.'

He was a man for whom 'duty' was written on a tablet of stone, Alvarez thought admiringly.

Dolores, her face glistening with sweat, came through from the kitchen and flopped down in one of the comfortable chairs. 'If it gets any hotter, I'll melt. Is it time for the news yet?' she asked, as she used her left foot to angle the fan more in her direction.

Alvarez looked at his watch. 'I'll switch on.'

Within a couple of minutes, the television news began. Initially, it was international in content and their interest was less than full—since the Peninsula was distant, what happened in Vietnam or Indonesia seemed of small account. But then it became not only national, but parochially so. The Prince and Princess of Wales, who were staying on the island as guests of the King and Queen, were due to sail on the Royal yacht, *Fortuna*, to watch the international dinghy races which were to be held in Llueso Bay. It was rumoured that one of the Royal princesses would be taking part . . .

'We must go and watch.' No one was a greater admirer of Royalty than Dolores.

Alvarez could not sleep. Was this a sign of imminent disaster—a ruptured appendix, strangled gut, heart attack, stroke? And then his circling, terrified thoughts swept him back to the television news and with a flash of inspiration he understood what was the motive for Gore's murder.

CHAPTER 20

To the obvious astonishment of the cabo on desk duty on Saturday morning, Alvarez arrived as the church clock was striking eight. He hurried up the stairs—too quickly, so that at the top he had to pause to regain his breath—and then sat behind his desk, dialled Tatham's number in England and when the connection was made, gave his name and asked to speak to the detective-superintendent.

'I'm afraid he's not in yet.'

'Not?' He'd imagined that a man of Tatham's calibre would be on duty at cock-crow.

'It's only just after seven, you know.'

He'd forgotten the hour's difference. 'When he arrives, will you ask him to phone me immediately? It's very important.'

After replacing the receiver, he stared at the top of the desk. If Salas accepted his report, then a massive security operation would begin in which he would have only a minor part to play. Yet for once such a thought gave him no pleasure. He wanted to be up and doing, working flat out to prevent the coming assassinations . . .

Eventually, Tatham rang.

'Señor, I am certain I know why Hickey was murdered. It was because the men who gave the orders to torture him into admitting his identity have decided on a new act of terror and this decision makes it obvious it was a bad mistake to leave him alive since he could recognize both them and his assailants.'

'What is the new plan?'

'King Juan Carlos and Queen Sofía have the Prince and Princess of Wales as guests on this island. At the end of

next week, they will be sailing on their yacht, *Fortuna*, to
Llueso Bay where there are to be international dinghy races
in which it is possible one of the princesses will be compet-
ing. I am certain that the intention is to assassinate the
Prince and Princess of Wales.'

'Jesus! Have you any idea what form their plan will take?'

'None, I'm afraid, beyond observing that it would seem
to be the most obvious thing to attempt to blow up the
Royal yacht.'

'Surely that's a threat your security forces face and meet
all the time?'

'Indeed. But you will know better than I that after a
while when nothing happens, security inevitably becomes
slacker.'

'And so a determined man with recycling scuba gear
could probably get under the yacht when it's at anchor or
hove to and plant an underwater bomb . . . All right, where
do we go from here?'

'I have to convince my superior chief of the fact that the
murder of Gore—I fear I keep thinking of him as Gore and
not Hickey—proves this threat is very real. To do that I
must tell him Liberation intended to assassinate the Prince
and Princess of Wales in England. Because you asked me
to keep that fact secret, I need your permission now to
break that confidence.'

'You have it. And when you speak to your superior chief,
tell him I will ensure he has every assistance from our end
that it's possible to give.'

Salas could act without prejudice when necessary. He
listened to Alvarez without once interrupting him, then
said: 'You've no hard proof that members of this terrorist
organization are intending to assassinate the visiting British
Royals?'

'No, señor.'

'But you say that the murder of Gore is inexplicable unless that is the case since no one else can have a motive for murdering him?'

'That is how I see things.'

'It makes sense. Can the English police name and describe the two members of Liberation who escaped arrest?'

'I am not certain on that point. I did not ask Señor Tatham earlier on as I thought it best if you spoke directly to him.'

'Quite so . . . Have you seen an itinerary of the Royal visit to Llueso Bay?'

'No, señor.'

'Nor have I. Obviously, Security will draw up a new itinerary and I'll see that a copy of this reaches you. They must mount a high profile operation and this will involve a large number of men. You will act as liaison officer. If accommodation has to be found, you will find it—I know this will be extremely difficult in the middle of the season, but if the worst comes to the worst, you will commandeer it. If extra telecommunications need to be installed, you will quote my authority for making certain they are provided immediately.'

'Yes, señor.'

'Have you anything more to add?'

'Just that when I spoke to Señor Tatham, he offered every possible assistance. Since the British will know how their own terrorists work, and presumably will be far more able to recognize them, perhaps from signs that we should miss, would it be an idea to ask them to send some men over to assist us?'

There was a long pause. 'Normally,' said Salas finally, 'there is no need for a Spaniard to seek help from anyone. However, the circumstances are not normal and there is reason in what you suggest. I shall put the point to whoever is placed in overall charge of security operations.'

*

Six British detectives from AT groups were flown in on Sunday morning and by the afternoon had begun to work with their Spanish counterparts. Language was a problem, but not an insuperable one; most of the Spaniards spoke English, one of the English actually spoke some Spanish, and Alvarez was there to help with translating.

Although it was judged most likely that the terrorists would base themselves in Puerto Llueso, the area to be searched was extended as far as Cala Beston since they might decide that in many ways it would be safer to be out of the area for most of the time, even if that meant risking repeated entries and exits. Every hotel was visited and registers and forward booking lists from travel companies examined; every rented villa and apartment was checked and the occupants questioned; hire car firms were made to open their books (their genuine books, not those prepared for the tax inspector) and provide lists of British hirers; yachtbrokers were asked for the names of British citizens who had chartered, or were booked to charter, a yacht or motorboat; firms who hired out diving equipment were questioned . . .

On Tuesday, there was a metaphorical bombshell. For the first time it was learned that the visiting Prince and Princess wanted to land in order to visit the caves, discovered earlier in the year, which had caused worldwide interest because of the colours in the stalactites and stalagmites and the fact that some of them had such complicated shapes they looked as if they'd been sculpted by hand. Security's reaction was predictable. On no account should any Royals land. The Spanish Royals reluctantly accepted the advice. The British Royals, with a blunt determination that was both applauded and condemned, rejected it on the grounds that to be seen to react so markedly to the threat would be to give Liberation a dangerous air of importance. A small price to pay for their safety, said Security; too great a price, said the British Royals.

More security men were drafted in from the Peninsula to strengthen and widen the search.

Alvarez yawned and waves of tiredness swept across his mind, yet, instead of slumping back in the chair and closing his eyes, he sat very upright and assured himself he would not fall asleep. It was astonishing behaviour.

He looked across his desk at the day-by-day calendar which, quite unusually, was up to date. Only twenty-six hours before *Fortuna* sailed into Llueso Bay. Yet all attempts to identify the terrorists had failed and, assuming they were in the area, they were free to pursue whatever form of terrorism they had planned. Before it had been known that the British Royals would land, the *Fortuna* would have been considered the prime target. But no longer. The moment the British Royals stepped ashore, they would be at risk; although they would be protected as well as could be, they could not be well protected. It was a maxim of security that if a terrorist were fanatical enough not to worry about his own life, there was no certain way to prevent him murdering his victim. He might shoot from very close range, throw a grenade, strap explosives about himself and become a human bomb, launch a rocket from a position from which there could be no escape; he might be a man of imagination and hire a helicopter which he armed with bombs . . .

Alvarez cursed his mind which produced ever more frightening possibilities and tried to think more constructively. It was often said that no crime was spontaneous. One could interpret that in more ways than one, but he took it to mean that there was no crime without a history and so to identify the history was to identify the crime . . .

He began to review everything which had happened from day one. He'd been ordered to Clinica Barón to speak to

Dr Molina and Señor Gore. Facts had suggested that Lady Macadie was committing adultery, but then had come the discovery that Gore was her half-brother, not her lover. Following that, the truth about Gore's torture had finally been admitted . . . Alvarez stopped his mind. Gore had lied about his identity; he had lied when he'd claimed to be Vivien Macadie's half-brother; why should he not also have been lying when he'd claimed the two intruders had tortured him in order to make him admit he was Townsend? What if they had known he was not because they were the two members of Liberation who had escaped capture and they had tortured him to discover what had happened to Townsend? Would this not indicate that, despite the fact it must have been far more dangerous for them to do the job themselves, they had been too scared of laying themselves open to betrayal or blackmail to employ hit men? Men so suspiciously careful would not hire professional killers to murder Gore, but would do it themselves. Yet the search over the past few days had failed to find them, so, accepting that the search had been thorough, it seemed they could not be in the area. Then had other members of the new Liberation, completely trustworthy because of their fanaticism, been given the task of carrying out the assassinations? But in this case, there would have been no need to murder Gore because he could not have recognized them . . .

Alvarez remembered something which, because the investigation into Gore's murder had not been in his hands, he'd forgotten until now. Gore had probably been about to pour drinks when he'd been killed. If any man would have been alert to danger, he would have been, yet it seemed he had perceived none. So his murderer could not have been one of the two men who had tortured him. And it was unlikely that the other could have been a member of a reformed Liberation because, after all that had happened,

Gore would have viewed any stranger with downright suspicion . . .

Contradictions. One moment the murderer had to be one of the original two, the next he couldn't have been; one minute Gore had to treat any stranger with frightened reserve, the next he'd been about to pour drinks . . .

Alvarez poured himself a drink; a large one. It seemed impossible to reconcile the contradictions and it would be easy to accept that therefore they had to be wrongly postulated. But remember the shepherds of years ago who'd taken their flocks up into the hills for the summer. If a lamb's missing, look for it either in the middle of your neighbour's flock or else somewhere where it's impossible for it to have gone. Most things that were called impossible were impossible only in the minds of the persons so naming them. The contradictions had to be capable of being reconciled. Somewhere, there had to be the key that would unlock the answer, just as a dislodged stone by a two-metre wall would show where the sheep had climbed. Where was the dislodged stone in this case?

The Spaniard! Detective-Superintendent Tatham had told him that a Spaniard had been arrested along with the other members of Liberation. Why had a Spanish terrorist allied himself with British terrorists unless . . .

He dialled Tatham's office.

'Have you had any luck?' Tatham asked eagerly.

'Not yet, señor.'

'Shit! When I heard it was you on the phone, I was hoping you'd either good news or another brainwave.'

'I do have an idea, but to call it anything more . . . I think I have found an inconsistency. Yet it may mean nothing, either because the world is full of inconsistencies or when all the facts are known it is no longer an inconsistency. Who was the Spaniard who was arrested with the other members of Liberation?'

'Ostensibly, a long-in-the-tooth student taking an English course. When arrested, he claimed that due to being too idealistic, he'd become mixed up with a group whose true aims had been hidden from him.'

'Do you remember his name and where he was born?'

'Not off-hand. Could those facts be significant?'

'They might well be.'

'Then I'll find out. It'll take time, so give me your number and I'll ring back.'

Alvarez replaced the receiver and wondered if he were making a fool of himself? Wouldn't Tatham have considered the possibility? But Tatham was used to the British character which was outward-looking; the Spanish character was inward-looking. Normally, no Spaniard would support a political group that did not have direct relevance to his own country and condition.

The phone rang. 'He was using false papers in the name of José Antonio Aguirre. He's refused to give any personal details and as far as the records show, no one in Spain has yet been able to establish his true identity.'

'That's it, then!'

'What's what and why the excitement?'

'José Antonio Aguirre was a Basque leader in the 'thirties who is still revered by many as one of the great leaders in the fight for independence. I think, señor, that the so-called student is a member of ETA and he assumed that name in honour of one of his heroes.'

'You're telling me I was had for a sucker when I accepted that he was just another fool idealist who'd been manipulated?'

'I may be totally wrong . . .'

'And you may be totally right. There have been rumours of loose tie-ups between terrorist organizations. And if you're thinking as you've got me thinking, it's a potentially fatal mistake to presume that the would-be assassin or

assassins in Puerto Llueso are British. They may well be
ETA members, doing Liberation's murderous work for
them because, ironically, a Basque national is likely to be
overlooked since there can be no discernible reason why
ETA should be concerned in the assassination of British
royalty . . . So what's the next move?'

'I shall speak to Superior Chief Salas. And perhaps you
would confer with him over the phone a little later on?'

'I'll get on to him in a quarter of an hour.'

Alvarez replaced the receiver, but did not immediately
telephone Palma. At long last, the facts slotted into place.
The two men who had previously tortured Gore, but
decided to let him alive, had returned to the island to make
contact with whoever was going to carry out the assassinations. While the odds were all against Gore's seeing them
and divining their motives, nevertheless life was forever
proving that statistical odds were liars. In any case, as
they'd shown previously, they were very, very careful. So,
seeing Gore's death as an insurance—overlooking the fact
that insurance revealed the need to insure—they had
arranged for his murder. The murderer had turned up at
Ca'n Renato, posing as a detective. With no reason to sus-
pect the truth, Gore had asked him into the house and
offered drinks . . .

CHAPTER 21

If Sargento Ortiz had not been so cynical that he believed every man guilty until he was proven guilty . . . If Herreros had not instinctively glanced at the outside door of the bar . . .

'Let's see your identity card.'

'I haven't got it on me,' Herreros mumbled. He looked as if his maker had become bored and careless when half way through making him.

'You're meant to carry it at all times. Where is it?'

'Back in my room.'

'What room?'

'At the hostal.'

'Where are you from?'

'Salamanca.'

'That's a bloody lie for a start. I was born in Alba. There's no Salamancan talks like you.'

'We . . . we moved when I was only a kid.'

'What are you doing on the island?'

'There aren't any jobs at home and I reckoned maybe I'd get work here.'

'Doing what?'

'I'm a waiter.'

'When did you arrive?'

'Four days ago.'

'So why come to Puerto Llueso?'

'Someone said that at this time of the year there was more chance of finding work here than around Palma.'

'That someone knows as much about the job market as I do about cow farming. You're a bloody liar,' Ortiz said for the second time. 'So we'll take a walk along to the post.'

Herreros, ever a fool, decided to make a break for it but, being no athlete, had reached no further than half way to the outside door when the muzzle of an automatic was pressed into the small of his back and he was promised a quick trip to hell if he took another step without orders.

Two men from Security and two from the Guardia searched Herreros's room at the Hostal Bahía. There, they found his identity card which showed he came from Tolosa, just over a hundred thousand pesetas, a cutting from *El Dia* which gave details of the Royal visit to Puerto Llueso and the caves, a 9mm Astra automatic and ten rounds of ammunition.

When faced with the evidence, he admitted with pride that it had been his intention to assassinate the Royals.

On Saturday, the lead story on the evening television was the arrival in Llueso Bay of the *Fortuna*, the dinghy race in which the Spanish princess had come second, and the visit to the caves by the Prince and Princess of Wales. The second story, held back for over twenty-four hours for security reasons, detailed the intended assassinations, foiled by the brilliant work of the combined forces of the Cuerpo General de Policías, the Guardia Civil, SIGC, and the Centre Superior para la Informacíon de la Defensa. Together, they had prevented a tragedy that would forever have blackened the name of Spain and they deserved to be honoured by every Spaniard . . .

'All because of you!' said Dolores excitedly.

'Not just me . . .' began Alvarez modestly.

The telephone rang. She went through to the front room, returned quickly. 'Señor Salas wishes to speak to you, Enrique.'

'At this time of night? What the hell's gone wrong now?'

'He's probably ringing to congratulate you.'

'And rabbits might mate with hedgehogs.'

He walked through to the front room, lifted the receiver, said: 'Señor?'

'Alvarez, I am not a man who normally favours superlatives, yet I now have no hesitation in saying that your work in this case deserves great praise. In the past, I may have had cause to complain about your undoubted propensity to complicate simple matters, but that you perceived the complications in this case was undoubtedly of advantage.

'I am told, though this must temporarily remain in confidence, that I am to receive congratulations from His Majesty in addition to those from the Prime Minister and the government. In these circumstances, I decided you should share in the pleasure of knowing the honour that such congratulations must bring me.'

'You are very kind, señor.'

'As I shall say to the very high official who will relay His Majesty's congratulations, I pride myself that when the honour of Spain was in my hands, I was not found wanting.'

'Far from wanting, señor.'

'Good night, Alvarez. Rest assured that I shall not forget that without your assistance it might well have taken longer to bring this case to so satisfactory a conclusion.' He rang off.

'Well?' asked Dolores, as Alvarez returned. 'Was he ringing to congratulate you?'

'I suppose so. Although he did seem to be congratulating himself rather more.'

'It's all so exciting I don't know what to do!'

'Have a drink to celebrate?' suggested Jaime.

Salas was a man of ambition and by the age of fifty it had been his intention to have become Director General of the Cuerpo General de Policía, from where it would be possible realistically to eye the highest positions of power in the land. It therefore came as a very unwelcome shock to discover that by fifty he might be not only unemployed, but also unemployable. 'It's impossible!' he shouted, forgetting that at such a moment it would have been better to project an image of cool, calm self-control.

'Not impossible. True.' Delgado had the generous paunch of someone who was both gourmet and gourmand. On first meeting, some were inclined to dismiss him as too eager to enjoy the pleasures of life to be of much consequence; if intelligent, they soon changed their minds and saw in the cold, fixed glint of the grey-blue eyes and the set of the mouth, the signs of hard, calculating authority.

'But it can't be true, señor,' Salas insisted, as if he believed that repeated denial might alter facts.

'I have been reliably assured that although Herreros comes from a family noted for its strong support of an independent Basque country, all attempts by him to join ETA have been rejected due to the fact that he is regarded as being both emotionally and mentally unstable.

'Recently, his novia told him she had decided she could never marry him and this made him even more unstable. He was heard to boast that he intended to do something that would prove both how wrong ETA had been to spurn him and change the course of history. He bought a nine-millimetre Astra from a well-known criminal, together with ammunition, and caught the ferry to this island on Wednesday. Yet he had no accomplices, no fixed plan of campaign, and is so totally unfamiliar with handguns that he has never actually fired one.'

'Then he could never have succeeded.'

'Precisely. Which is why I'm here now. In the face of so absurd a threat, the massive counter-measures which were taken by us appear totally ridiculous.'

'But . . . but we didn't know it was like that.'

'Pull yourself together, man. The public has been told

that ETA mounted a dangerously cunning attempt to assassinate the visiting Royals and this was only foiled by the cleverness of our security forces who, in recognition of their brilliance, have been congratulated by everyone from His Majesty down to the politicians. What do you imagine will be the public's reaction if it learns that the attempt was conceived by a half-witted youth and couldn't have succeeded if nine-tenths of the army of security men had been fast asleep?'

Salas flapped his hands.

Delgado leaned forward. 'The public will laugh, loud and long, at both the security forces and all those who have been so lavish with their praise. What does a politician do when he's being laughed at?'

'God knows.'

'One does not have to be that omniscient. He vents his bile. And since you have maintained a very high profile in this case . . . Need I say more?'

Salas made a sound that was a cross between a moan and a groan.

'I imagine that you will agree that a damage-limiting exercise needs to be undertaken?'

Salas was too disturbed to agree or disagree with anything.

'Herreros proudly admits it was his intention to murder the Royals and so he can be convicted without the need of a full trial and publicity can be kept to a minimum. The Press can be further muzzled in the name of security. Should ETA deny Herreros was a member, this can be countered by the claim that they are trying with false denials to conceal their chagrin at failure . . . So, provided there are no slip-ups, we can rely on the fact that there will be a sufficiency of wars, famines, earthquakes, murders, and financial scandals, in the world to make the public quickly lose all interest in the intended assassinations. But nothing, nothing whatsoever, must occur which might restore that interest.' Delgado stood. 'It is no exaggeration to say that your professional future rests on the public's ignorance being maintained.'

Salas escorted him through the outer office to the lift, then returned to slump down in his chair and gaze vacantly at the far wall. Above his head hung Damocles's sword. Let the first hint of the truth surface . . . 'Oh my God!' Alvarez who believed Gore had been murdered in order to facilitate the assassination was trying to identify the murderer and in his bumbling, incompetent hands . . .

He dialled Alvarez's number, but replaced the receiver after the first ring. Gore *had* been murdered. So who had murdered him if there had been no assassination plot? He dialled Fiol's number, to be informed that the inspector was away from the office, pursuing inquiries into the murder of the English señor. Salas kicked the desk in a childish expression of rage.

'You tried to get in touch with me, señor?' said Fiol, over the phone.

'What's happening in the murder investigation?'

'I'm afraid that matters are a little confused . . .'

'Don't use that blasted word.'

Fiol was bewildered. 'I . . . I don't understand . . .'

'Have you discovered who shot the Englishman?'

'Unfortunately, there is so little solid evidence. I have heard from the laboratory, but as you'll have noted from the copy of the report sent to you, that doesn't really help.'

Salas had been far too busy receiving congratulations to read reports. 'What progress have you made in the field?'

'I have questioned neighbours and villagers, but so many of them are antagonistic, deficient in intelligence, or both, that their evidence is useless. I've tried to establish the motive for the murder, but to date without success. In the light of this, had there been valuables missing, it would have been reasonable to assume the murder was carried out by an opportunist thief, interrupted by the señor. However, the Sitzar woman claims that nothing is missing.'

'Then she's mistaken. Being a foreigner, the señor must have had large sums in cash; he'll have kept these hidden, from her as much as from anyone else. That is what's been stolen.'

'Naturally, I have not overlooked the possibility, señor, but there is no evidence to support it. Of course, it is true that as there's no other discernible motive . . .'

'Since clearly this case is unlikely to be brought to a successful conclusion, there can be no justification for spending more time on it.'

Fiol was eager to prove himself. 'I suggest that if I just keep pegging away at it, I may . . .'

'You'll never reach higher rank if you don't learn to take the broad view. If the chance of success in any case becomes too small, there can be no justification for pursuing the investigation.'

Fiol couldn't fathom why Salas was for once content to accept failure, but he did know that a superior's wishes were his command. 'I understand perfectly, señor.'

Salas rang off. Then he remembered something and dialled the number again. 'On no account will you suffer interference in this case from any other quarter, least of all from Inspector Alvarez.'

'You may rely on me to make certain of that,' Fiol replied, a note of satisfaction in his voice.

CHAPTER 22

Alvarez stared through the unshuttered window at the soft drizzle which had been falling for the past half-hour. The air in the fields would be filled with the magic smell of earth which had received the first rain of the autumn . . .

The phone range. 'What the devil do you mean by ignoring my orders?' was Salas's greeting.

'Ignoring which orders, señor?'

'To cease interfering in Inspector Fiol's investigations into the murder of the Englishman. How dare you ask the laboratory what calibre bullet was used.'

'It's only that I was curious to discover if Señor Gore had been shot with the gun in Herreros's possession . . .'

'That does not concern you. It is not your case.'

'Yet knowing it's virtually certain Herreros was the murderer . . .'

'He did not arrive on the island until six days after the Englishman was killed.'

'He . . . he didn't?'

'I presume that even you can now appreciate that he could not have committed the murder?'

'But then if he didn't kill the señor, who did?'

'Inspector Fiol, who has conducted a most rigorous investigation, is of the firm opinion that the murderer was an opportunist thief, surprised in the middle of his theft.'

'That's impossible. Señor Gore had begun to pour out a drink for his visitor.'

'Why the devil do you say that?'

'On the floor was a broken glass, which had contained whisky, and on top of the cocktail cabinet was another glass with whisky in it, a bottle of whisky, and a soda siphon.'

'Where's that evidence from? There's been none such in any of Fiol's reports.'

'There hasn't? . . . Of course, it was Aguenda who told me and I don't suppose she mentioned it to him. She tidied everything away, not realizing how that could affect the investigation. My reading would be that the señor had poured out the two whiskies and was about to add soda when he was shot.'

'And my reading of your reading is that once again you're damned well trying to complicate everything. Are you incapable of understanding that a simple answer is usually the correct one? Clearly, the señor poured himself a drink, dropped the glass by mistake, and was about to add soda to a second one when he was interrupted.'

'But, señor—'

'Goddamit, be quiet! This is a murder without any obvious motive. That points irresistibly to the fact that it was fortuitous. The thief was searching for the cash which had to be hidden in the house. The señor interrupted him and was shot. Inspector Fiol is a man never content to admit failure, but even he is ready to accept that in the circumstances the chances of indentifying the murderer are slight indeed. Were you to interfere further, even that chance would undoubtedly vanish. I therefore forbid you to have anything more to do with the case. You will not go within a thousand kilometres of Altobarí. Is that clear?' Salas rang off.

Alvarez came to his feet and crossed to the window; the drizzle had ceased and road and pavements were steaming. He wished he possessed the intelligence to make sense of events. The discovery of the assassination plot had come about as a result of Gore's death, yet Salas was now saying that it had been a motiveless murder and totally unconnected with Liberation—how could that be? Gore surely had poured out two whiskies and he'd only have done that if there were a visitor whom he knew or had no reason to fear. Who could that someone be? Why hadn't he, with every reason to be wary, not had the slightest suspicion he could be in danger?

And then Alvarez remembered that when he'd returned from England, he'd lazed away the rest of the day instead of pursuing his investigations as a keen and ambitious detective would have done.

Enriqueta let him into the house. 'Are the señor and señora at home?' he asked.

'Yes, but she's still in bed.' She looked at him, a sly smile lurking around the corners of her mouth.

'Because she's pregnant?'

Her surprise was immediate. 'How did you know that?'

'Call it an inspired guess. Well, if she's hors de combat, will you tell the señor I'd like a word with him?'

She left him in the sitting-room and in less than a minute, Macadie entered. 'Good afternoon, Inspector. Do sit down and may I offer you coffee or tea?'

How could any man control his outward emotions so completely? Alvarez wondered. 'Thank you, señor, but I won't have anything.'

'Do you think we've had enough rain to do some good?'

'Not yet, but once the weather breaks there's usually quite a bit more rain before the sun returns ... Señor, I have to ask some questions and these may offend you. Please believe me when I say I much regret this. Is the señora pregnant?'

'Yes.'

'Was Señor Gore the father?'

Macadie looked as if he had been dealt a blow that had suddenly emptied his lungs. In the ensuing silence, a clock struck the hour. 'Then you know?' he asked flatly.

'I think so.'

'But do you understand?'

'I'm not certain.'

'Have you any love for the land?'

'I come from peasant stock and so if I could, I would buy a large finca and spend the rest of my life serving it. For me, the feel of rich earth is more exciting than a woman's breast . . . Forgive me for such crudity.'

'I couldn't have put it more aptly . . . In England, I own an estate and every time I walk the fields, I feel both proud and humble, owner and yet mere trustee. If a Macadie is in possession in two thousand and sixty-eight, some of the land will have been in the family for a thousand years. Could any man not be both thrilled and humbled by such knowledge?'

'Not one who understands the truth about life.'

'When one has been entrusted with history, one must dedicate oneself to preserving it. I married for the first time in the hopes that my wife would bear the son who would himself, or through his son, usher in the thousand years. So when she failed to conceive, I persuaded her we should seek advice. Tests were begun, but eventually she refused to continue them, finding the necessary examinations abhorrent. I was naturally extremely disappointed, but accepted the decision since it was caused by feelings beyond her control. My tests, however, were completed and later these showed that I was infertile with no possibility, under contemporary medical knowledge, of having that fertility restored. I could not have an heir.

'My first wife died in a riding accident. I thought I was too old to consider remarrying, but we have a saying: There's no fool like an old fool. When a charming, considerably younger woman makes it obvious that she finds one attractive . . .

'Initially, when I learned about Vivien's friendship with Gore, I was deeply hurt; but as you know, almost immediately she explained that he was her half-brother. I up-braided myself for my disgraceful lack of faith, never mind how briefly it had lasted, and set out to make up for it in so far as that was possible. But I just could not bring myself to like Gore. In the end, I had to console my conscience with the thought that provided I didn't show my dislike, this fact really was unimportant. Which attitude sufficed until I learned that she was pregnant . . .

'Throughout history, there have been cuckolded hus-bands who discover that the children their wives are carry-ing are not theirs. In the old days, when values were sharper and crueller, most husbands either killed their wives or threw them out of the house, but even then there must have been some who had reason publicly to accept the children as their own. I think that in different circumstances I could calmly have accepted Vivien's child as my own. If I did, there was every chance there would be a Macadie living in Stowton Place in two thousand and sixty-eight and only Vivien and I, long since dead, would have known that he was a lie and that the Macadies had failed to reach their millennium. After all, the older one gets, the clearer one sees that there are times when the lie is to be preferred to the truth. But Gore wasn't just her lover, he was her half-brother . . .'

Alvarez mopped the sweat from his forehead; sweat that, in the air-conditioned room, had nothing to do with heat.

'I saw it as my duty to kill him because I believed that only then could I guarantee that no one else would ever learn that the estate must one day belong to the child of an incestuous union. When I arrived at his villa, he guessed I knew, but not what was my intention. He began obsequi-ously to try to divert my anger and hatred with a flood of words and prepared to pour out drinks; but when he began to excuse himself on the grounds that it was as much Vivien's fault as his own, I produced the gun. He panicked.

He swore he wasn't Vivien's brother and so the relationship hadn't been incestuous. It's easier to shoot a liar than an honest man; a coward than a brave man.' Macadie was silent for a while, then he added: 'I killed him in order to hide the truth. Of course, I have merely made certain that the truth has to come to light.'

'Señor, there is one thing you should know. When he claimed he was not your wife's brother, that was the truth. His name was Sydney Hickey, a criminal, who was at the rehabilitation centre at the same time as Franklin Gore. He murdered Señor Gore because Señor Gore was unwise enough to reveal to him the facts that a large sum of money was waiting for him and that his sister had married a very wealthy man. Hickey came to this island hoping to make more money through the señora. Sadly, a relationship developed between them. Then, when it was so unexpectedly disclosed by me, the señora took the only course that was open to her to conceal the truth.'

'Oh my God!' Macadie leaned his head forward and covered his face with his hands. 'In God's name, why couldn't you have told me this in time?' He uncovered his face, straightened up. 'Will you allow me to speak to my wife before arresting me?'

'I intend to do no more than ask you for your passport, señor. Inspector Fiol is the officer in charge and therefore it is up to him to take further action.'

Macadie stood. 'I'll get it for you.' He took a couple of steps, came to a stop. 'Will my motive for killing him have to be made public?'

'Señor, as a detective, I have to answer that the truth must be given. As a man, it occurs to me that if you make it clear to Inspector Fiol that you were never hoodwinked by the lie that Señor Gore was your wife's half-brother, but did not name it a lie immediately because you were desperately trying to make the parties break off the relationship in order that your marriage could be saved . . . Then I cannot see why anyone else should ever know.'

'Apart from you?'

'I have always hoped that I am a man before I am a detective.'

Alvarez reluctantly dialled the number. 'Yes?' said Fiol.

'I've uncovered fresh evidence in the murder case which shows that the murder wasn't committed by a casual thief.'

'All that I have uncovered points unambiguously to the fact that it was.'

'But what I have to tell you . . .'

'The superior chief made it crystal clear that I am to reject any attempt by you to interfere further in this case.'

'I don't think one can really call what I have to tell you an interference . . .'

'I can think of no other word that is relevant. Is that all?'

'In the circumstances, perhaps it is.'

'Good.' He cut the connection.

Alvarez scratched his chin. Consequences in life never ceased to astonish him. If he hadn't been so determined to prove Flores's innocence of one crime, despite his un-doubted guilt of untold others . . . If he hadn't uncovered Vivien Macadie's adultery . . . If he hadn't decided it was necessary to go to England . . . If on his return from there he hadn't been so lazy as to while away the rest of the day instead of driving up to Son Termol to tell Macadie that while Hickey was his wife's lover, he was not her half-brother . . . If Hickey had not been murdered, so that the false connection between his murder and the assassination plot had not been made . . .

There were still one or two points which puzzled him. No one other than Herreros had been arrested, yet all security investigation had ceased. Since he must have had consider-able back-up, one would have expected Security to continue

the search to identify those concerned . . . But as Guillermo
Ibañez had written in the nineteenth century: Have pity for
the man who discovers all the answers, for then he can have
no questions.

Alvarez decided a small celebration was in order. He
opened the bottom right-hand drawer of the desk and with-
drew the bottle of Soberano and a glass.